HETTY'S HIGHWAYMAN

Hetty Neville, a tomboy, steals a ride on a hay cart with her friend Ned. Then she meets Will Foster and discovers the first stirrings of love, but Will hides a secret. Highwaymen are in the area, robbing travellers, and he and Ned are implicated. Hetty's stepfather is the magistrate, sworn to hang all highwaymen caught, but Hetty is prepared to do whatever it takes to save them from the trap her stepfather has set.

ELIZABETH STEVENS

HETTY'S
HIGHWAYMAN

Complete and Unabridged

LINFORD
Leicester

First published in 2005 in Great Britain

First Linford Edition
published 2005

British Library CIP Data

Stevens, Elizabeth
  Hetty's highwayman.—Large print ed.—
Linford romance library
  1. Love stories
  2. Large type books
  I. Title
  823.9'14 [F]

  ISBN 1–84617–107–5

Published by
F. A. Thorpe (Publishing)
Anstey, Leicestershire
Set by Words & Graphics Ltd.
Anstey, Leicestershire
Printed and bound in Great Britain by
T. J. International Ltd., Padstow, Cornwall

This book is printed on acid-free paper

1

'Hetty, I can see for miles up here! All the way to the main road! I could see the post coach coming a mile off, earn a penny letting them know at the inn before they hear the horn!'

The boy, standing on the thick, out-jutting branch of the larch tree, fifteen feet from the ground, called down eagerly to his companion below. Hetty Neville was hopping excitedly from foot to foot.

'What else can you see, Ned?'

'Oh, lots of things! I can see right over the tops of the hedges, into the fields. I reckon I can see right across the main road, nearly as far as Ruscombe church.'

'I want to see, too! Help me up, Ned!'

Hetty set her foot on the first outjutting stone of the wall that ran alongside the big tree. Below the wall, on the far side, a narrow lane led past the boundary of the Lattimore estate.

'But you're a lass!' Ned glanced down at her in surprise. 'You can't climb trees!'

'Can't I? Just watch me!' Hetty bent down and reached for the hem at the back of her skirt, pulling it up between her legs and tucking it into the waist at the front, making a rather baggy pair of breeches.

She kicked off her shoes and, in her stockinged feet, began to scramble up to the top of the wall, following the route she had just watched Ned take.

From the top of the wall she reached out and grasped one of the tree's smaller branches, hauling herself upwards until she reached the branch overhanging the lane, where Ned was standing.

She scrambled up beside him, sitting on the branch with her back against the main trunk. Ned was standing beside her, steadying himself with a hand on the trunk, his bare toes gripping the branch.

'It's higher up here than I've ever been, except when I've been in the attics at the Hall,' Hetty said. It took a moment to pluck up the courage to look down at the ground, but then she quickly looked away again, over the fields towards the roofs of the village cottages in the distance, resolutely determined not to look down at the lane again.

'Reckon I haven't climbed higher than this before,' Ned said, shifting his feet to a more stable position. 'Reckon we should mark the occasion so that anyone else who climbs this high will know that we did it first.'

'How do you mean, Ned?' Hetty asked.

'Move over a bit and let me come up close to the trunk,' he said. Hetty sat down on the branch, which felt safer, but still kept hold of the trunk. Ned edged his way along until he was standing beside her and close to the trunk. He took out his pocketknife and began carving into the bark.

'What are you doing?' She craned her neck to see.

'Got to scrape away this rough bark first, make a smooth bit so what's carved here will show up, stay for ever.'

'Let me see!'

Ned was blocking her view and Hetty couldn't see what he was doing without moving precariously along the branch. She had to wait impatiently while Ned worked, but at last he stopped, blew away a few loose pieces of wood, and moved back along the branch so that she could see his work.

'H.N. and N.F. 1720,' she read. 'Ned, that's beautiful! Now, anyone else who climbs up here will know we did it first!'

'It'll last as long as the tree stands, and I reckon that'll be a good few years more,' Ned said with satisfaction. 'I'd have liked to put our full names, but I'm not too good about words and besides, there wasn't space.'

'If I'm still living at Birch Hall when I'm an old lady I'll tell all the village children and maybe they'll want to climb up and see for themselves.'

'All your grandchildren, perhaps.' Ned Laughed. 'And mayhap my grandchildren will be the ones climbing up to see it.'

'Look, there's a haycart coming along the lane,' Hetty said, pointing. Beyond the bend they could see a cart, piled high with hay, coming slowly towards them, pulled by an ancient grey carthorse. The driver was sitting on one of the shafts, leaning against the side of the cart. He looked half asleep in the warm heat of the late summer afternoon.

'Let's take a ride on it,' Ned said suddenly.

'But he'd never let us.' Hetty objected.

'He won't even notice. Look, when it passes beneath us, drop on to the top of the hay. It's so high it won't be more than a few feet below this branch.'

Hetty looked down and had to tighten her grip on the trunk. It looked a fearsome distance between here and the ground, and if they missed . . .

'We won't miss.' Ned read the expression on her face. 'That load's so wide it fills the lane. When I say, just drop. Step off the branch and we'll fall right into a nice, soft bed of hay.'

The cart was coming nearer, the horse ambling tiredly as it pulled the heavy load, the driver's head lolling from side to side as he dozed.

'Now!' Ned jumped as he spoke, and Hetty shut her eyes tightly and stepped off the branch at the same instant. Almost at once she felt herself enveloped in the warm, sweet-smelling hay and realised they'd hardly dropped more than her own height. She lay still, almost buried in the hay, and was conscious of Ned's hand reaching out to clasp hers.

'See? Easy, wasn't it? And it's a lovely soft couch. I wish my bed at home was as good.'

Ned lived in one of the cottages in the village with his mother, a widow who took in washing and cleaned the rooms at the local inn in order to feed and clothe them both.

Hetty had known Ned most of her life. When her father had died they had been very poor, and if it had not been for Mary Fletcher's kindness in offering to share her cottage with them, they might have fared very ill. But fortunes had changed for Hetty and her mother Margaret in the last few years.

By chance, Margaret had met an old friend of her late husband at the home of a distant cousin, in Maidenhead. Sir John Lattimore was wealthy and an important man in the county, a local magistrate and Justice of the Peace.

He had at once been attracted to the still young and pretty widow and within six months had married Margaret and taken her and her daughter to live at Birch Hall, his country estate, which happened to be on the outskirts of the village where they had lived in poverty after Hetty's father's untimely death.

Sir John was a kindly man, treating

Hetty as though she were his own daughter, but he was known throughout the county as a stern judge, the terror of all the local poachers and petty felons. Sir John's greatest venom, however, was directed against the local highwaymen, armed men who held up coaches travelling through the area, robbing the occupants and on occasion, shooting anyone bold enough, or foolish enough, to show defiance.

* * *

The village straddled the Bath Road, the main thoroughfare out of London to the west. It was a busy route, with a thrice daily coach service plus all the mail coaches, to say nothing of the private vehicles of the wealthy, who wished to travel to Bath for the purposes of taking the waters or enjoying the gaiety of the annual season, or merchants travelling to Bristol to trade out of the port, as well as those making shorter journeys to

Marlborough or Chippenham.

If the coaches came safely through Hounslow Heath, an area just to the west of London and so notorious for highwaymen that there were gibbets put up by the roadside where convicted robbers hung in cages as a warning to others, then the next most dangerous place on the route was Maidenhead thicket, where the road passed through dense woodland, the perfect place for a robber's ambush.

Sir John had vowed to hang any highwayman caught, but so far their cunning and bravado had eluded all efforts of the constabulary to bring them to justice, or even to discover their identity, while coaches were still being held up and robbed with a depressing frequency.

★   ★   ★

The haycart made its slow way down the lane, the load swaying as the tired horse ambled between the shafts. Hetty sat up, pushing hay from her hair and face, and found Ned beside her, lying on his stomach and looking over the edge of the load.

'I reckon we're as high as a house roof up here,' he said, gazing down at the hedges below them. 'The load's too big for this cart. Reckon they're in a hurry to get all the harvest in before the weather breaks.'

'Ned, be careful you don't make it tip over.' Hetty grabbed his hand.

'Nay. Take more'n my weight to rock this load.' All the same, he wriggled further towards the centre of the cart, burrowing into the warm nest.

'How far do you think we'll be going?' Hetty raised her head to look down the lane. It was fun to ride up here, but she'd have to walk back in stockinged feet. It was all very well for Ned, he mostly went barefoot.

'We'll likely be going to the big barn in the field at the bottom of the lane,' Ned said. 'Not much farther. Look, we're slowing for the turn now.'

The driver had climbed down from his perch on the shafts and taken the horse's bridle, leading him through a gap in the hedge into a fallow field. Nearby stood a high barn, roofed but open at the sides. The horse brought his load right up to the side of the barn, then, with the driver's help, backed the load inside. Hetty and Ned found themselves close to the cross beams which formed the underside of the roof.

'How do we get down?' she whispered.

Almost at once her question was answered when a great heap of hay fell from under them, sliding like a waterfall from the cart on to the floor of the barn. Hetty felt herself drop several feet, but stayed in the cart. Ned, however, was nearer the back, and as the cart continued to disperse its load he slid with it, rolling over and over, finally landing on the barn floor on top of a heap of hay. He struggled to sit up, seeing to his dismay that several men were gathered round, staring at him, all holding menacing-looking pitchforks.

'What have we here, then?' said one of them, his gaitered legs no more than two feet from Ned's face. 'Big sort of fieldmouse to pick up with the load!'

Ned had been winded by the abrupt fall, but he tried to scramble to his feet. The faces looking down at him seemed disconcertingly unfriendly.

'What you doin' in my 'aycart, then?' one of them asked roughly. It was the owner of the gaitered legs and, looking up, Ned saw that it was Abel Benson, the foreman at the farm where the hay had been delivered. The other men he knew by sight but not well enough to hope that they might be friendly towards him.

'I only wanted a ride,' he said meekly. He tried to get to his feet but one of Benson's boots kicked him in the back of his legs and sent him sprawling back on to the hay.

Benson stood over him menacingly. 'A ride! 'Ow d'you get up on top there, then?'

'I dropped off a branch.'

'Like a ripe plum!' sneered one of the men.

'Liar! There ain't no trees in ten acre field!' Benson aimed another kick at Ned. 'Well, lads,' he looked round at the other men. 'Seems we caught a little animal in with our 'ay. What shall we do with him, eh?'

Laughing, the men closed in round Ned. Probably, most of them would have let him go with no more than a clout round his ear, but Benson was out for some amusement and none of them was prepared to argue with their foreman.

Ned made a sudden dash towards a gap in the circle of men. Someone stuck out a pitchfork and he tripped, causing them to laugh.

'I think this young feller-me-lad needs teaching a lesson,' Benson said. 'Learn 'im not to go riding in 'aycarts where he's no business to be.'

'Why shouldn't I?' Ned retorted, with a show of defiance. 'I wasn't stealing your wretched hay. How could I? What harm was it to take a ride?'

'Ho! He's a bold one! Bold young lads need to be taught to respect their elders.' Benson grinned round at the other men, then, very slowly, he undid his belt and let it dangle from his hand. Ned saw that the buckle end, heavy metal with a spike on it, was swinging loose. Benson wound the other end round his hand.

Without warning, he swung the belt and struck at Ned. The spike caught him on the side of his face and a trickle of blood ran down his cheek.

'Let's see how bold you are after a good thrashing with this 'ere belt!' Benson swung the belt again, catching Ned across his head. Ned backed away, but the circle was closing in and Benson was now standing over him.

It wasn't by any means the first time in his short life that Ned had experienced the feel of a leather belt on his skin, but Benson's belt was worse than anything he'd known before.

Where was Hetty, Ned wondered. He hoped she'd have the sense to stay hidden amongst the hay if she could, and wait until the men had moved away. Benson might not actually strike her, if he realised who she was, but he'd certainly be unpleasant and she was better off staying out of sight.

Benson kicked him again, then raised his arm to strike a third blow, when suddenly the rest of the hay cascaded down from the uptipped cart, bringing Hetty sailing down with it, to land on top of the pile, beside Ned. Benson, startled, stepped back a pace and Hetty leapt to her feet, shouting furiously.

'Benson — you can stop that at once! You've no call to beat the boy, or do you intend to thrash me as well?' She pulled at the hem of her skirt, still tucked into her waistband, and shook it down, brushing pieces of hay off it. She glared at Benson.

'Well, well! Seems we've more'n one of 'em stealing a ride! And a little lass, too, who ought to know better than to get up to such rough goings-on.'

'Benson! Do you know who I am?' Hetty put her hands on her hips and stared defiantly at the foreman. She hoped she didn't look as dishevelled as she felt.

'I know who you be,' Benson said slowly. 'You be Sir John's ward, but what you be doin' in a 'aycart when you oughter be at home learning how to be a proper lady, I don't know.'

'I'm Sir John's step-daughter,' Hetty said haughtily. 'And it's no business of yours if I should choose to take a ride in a haycart. It's Sir John's hay, after all.'

Benson laughed nastily. 'Fiery little wench, ain't yer? Do Sir John know what you get up to with the village lads?'

'And does Sir John know about what you get up to, at nights, poaching rabbits?' Hetty snapped back. She had the great satisfaction of seeing Benson look discomfited. 'I should remind you, Benson, that snaring rabbits on private property is a criminal offence, riding in a haycart is not. Which do you think Sir John would be more interested in hearing about?'

' 'Ow d'you know . . . ?' For a moment, Benson's jaw dropped, before he decided to bluff his way out.

Seizing her advantage, Hetty grabbed Ned's arm and pulled him to his feet. 'Come on, Ned. We mustn't hold up unloading the hay any longer.'

She dragged him towards the side of the barn and to her relief, the men blocking their way instinctively fell back to let them pass.

They kept on walking, out of the barn and round the side of it, towards the gap in the hedge. Behind them they heard guffaws of laughter from the men, but whether it was at Benson's expense or because of her, Hetty neither knew nor cared.

'How did you know Benson had been poaching rabbits?' Ned asked curiously when they were safely outside the barn.

'I didn't. But I know now. It's the

sort of thing someone like him would do, so I took a chance and it looked as if I guessed right and worried him. I don't think he'll say anything to Sir John about us being on the haycart.'

As they rounded the hedge into the lane they nearly bumped into someone just entering the field.

'Hey, steady, lass!' He put out a hand to prevent Hetty cannoning into him. 'It's my guess you've been sent off by Benson with a flea in your ears. He doesn't like anyone meddling in his hay barns.'

'We were only taking a ride on one of the carts as it passed along the lane, Will,' Ned explained. He seemed to know the man, although Hetty had never seen him before.

He was youngish, and pleasant faced, dressed like a farmer but not in the rough working clothes of a labourer. She didn't think he looked as if he was going to give them another telling off, even if the hay turned out to be his, not Sir John's.

'A ride on the haycart? And did the driver not object?' Will asked.

'He didn't know. We were on the top of the pile, way above his head. He was dozing on the shafts, anyway,' Ned replied.

'On top of the hay? How could you do that? Did someone toss you up there on the end of a pitchfork?' Will's eyebrows were raised in surprise.

'We dropped from the branch of the larch tree that overhangs the lane,' Hetty explained, feeling foolish. She would have liked to appear grown-up and ladylike in front of this man, but, barefoot and with her dress crumpled and full of bits of straw, she knew she must look like a labourer's child.

'And whom do I have the pleasure of addressing?' Will asked, giving her a bow. 'Ned, you have not introduced me to your companion.'

Hetty wasn't sure whether he was making fun of her or not.

'I'm Hetty Neville, from Birch Hall,' she said, before Ned could speak.

'Mistress Neville? Surely, you are not Sir John's ward?' Will asked.

'Not ward, exactly. I'm his step-daughter.' Hetty hoped he wasn't going to tell Sir John about the haycart. He looked friendly enough, but one could never be sure, especially if he was a neighbour and friend of St John.

'Well, Mistress Hetty Neville, let me introduce myself. I am Will Foster, and I own a small farm to the south of here. May I say I feel greatly honoured to meet a lady who mounts haycarts from the branch of a tree? It must have been a very high branch and took some skill in climbing, to say nothing of the courage to drop off it on to the cart. Had you given any thought to the consequences had you misjudged the timing and missed the cart?'

He wasn't laughing at her now.

Hetty said frankly, 'I didn't give it a thought at the time, but now, I don't think I want to dwell on the possibility.'

Will nodded. 'And neither do I,' he said quietly.

Ned interrupted eagerly, 'The branch makes an excellent lookout, Will! You can see all the way to Ruscombe church from there! See the mail coach coming from miles away, and a great many other things, too!'

'I've no doubt. But, Ned, may I suggest you forget about climbing trees for today and go home and have that cut on your cheek bathed? You look like an escaped felon with your face torn and blood all over your shirt.'

Ned grinned. 'I'm all right,' he muttered. ' 'Tis nothing much, though if I'd known Benson was in such a foul mood I don't reckon I'd have risked riding down to the barn.'

'No doubt he wanted to impress the hired hands. Maybe he wouldn't have struck you so viciously if he'd been on his own.' Will turned to Hetty. 'Take him off and see that he cleans those cuts, Mistress Hetty.' He gave her a second bow. 'I hope we may meet again, although I beg you, do not drop on me from a tree branch when I'm riding beneath.' He moved away into the field, towards where a brown horse stood waiting, patiently cropping the grass.

'You'd better go home and ask Mistress Fletcher to bathe those cuts,' Hetty said abruptly. 'He's right, you do look like a runaway convict, with all that blood over your shirt.'

' 'Tis nothing much. Benson doesn't scare me,' Ned said stoutly. He wasn't going to admit, even to Hetty, his best friend, that he had been frightened.

They walked slowly up the lane towards the gages of Birch Hall, Ned limping slightly and Hetty finding it painful, treading on the loose stones in her stockinged feet.

At the gates they parted, Ned to plod on to his mother's cottage in the village, Hetty to retrieve her shoes from under the tree and to slip back into the house by a side door and tidy herself before anyone saw her.

'Benson really thought you knew about his poaching. He must have been doing a lot of it,' Ned remarked as they stood talking for a moment.

'And probably taking deer, too,' Hetty said. 'Perhaps he'll stop now, if he thinks he's likely to be reported.'

Ned shook his head. 'No. More likely he'll learn to be more cautious, more cunning. Benson isn't the kind of person to be scared off easily. You wouldn't tell Sir John about him, would you?'

'No, I wouldn't. But that's because I haven't any proof, not because I have any sympathy for Benson. My stepfather wouldn't be able to do anything just because I told him Benson looked guilty when it was suggested. He's a magistrate and a Justice of the Peace; he has to be just and fair to everyone, even criminals.'

'More's the pity,' Ned muttered.

'Tell Mistress Fletcher to see to those cuts!' Hetty called, as Ned shambled off along the lane, still limping slightly. 'There's blood all over the back of your hair. Best not mention the haycart to her, say you fell out of a tree.'

Ned nodded but he knew his pride wouldn't let him admit to falling out of a tree, he was the best tree climber in the county. But then, he wasn't going to tell his mother he'd been beaten by Benson, either. That wouldn't be wise.

He trudged on round the bend in the lane, out of Hetty's sight without looking back, though he knew she was still standing at the gate, watching him.

2

Hetty rescued her shoes and slipped into the house unobserved. She was sitting reading demurely in her bedroom when she heard her mother calling her.

'Hetty! Where are you? I've been looking everywhere for you!'

'Here, Mama. I was in the garden earlier.' It wasn't exactly a lie, Hetty had been in the garden before the haycart incident. Fortunately, Margaret Lattimore was too eager to impart her news to be concerned about her daughter's other whereabouts.

'Such news, Hetty! Such excitement! Sir John has just told me he is planning a party here at the Hall, in two weeks' time, and all his friends from London will be coming down for it! I expect the majority of them will stay overnight, so we have to start at once to plan where everyone is to sleep.'

'A party? Why, what for?' Hetty asked. Sir John was not the most sociable of men, even though he was well-known in the village and beyond, in the towns of Maidenhead, and even Reading.

'Well, it's for two reasons, actually.' Margaret looked a little coy as she answered. 'Sir John wanted to entertain his friends among the justiciary and thank them for all their help in his elevation to the Bench, as Magistrate.'

'Oh.'

Hetty was disappointed. If it was all Sir John's legal friends, they would be a dull, elderly lot. Hetty would be expected to help entertain but it was bound to be a tedious occasion.

'But that's not all!' Margaret's face glowed as she imparted her real news. 'Sir John has long been thinking that it was time he gave some thought to your future, my dear. He wants you to make a good marriage to some worthy and honourable man, and so he is inviting several suitable gentlemen, sons of friends of his, to dine with us that evening, and, who knows, there might be someone amongst them with whom you might feel you could make a happy alliance.'

'Marriage! Me!' Hetty said, shocked. 'But, Mama, I'm only sixteen! Surely it's far too early to think of such things yet!'

'My dear, sixteen is the ideal age to begin thinking of marriage. And I must say, now that the subject has come up, that I feel it is high time that you began to behave like a young lady, less like a hoyden.

'What are people going to think of you, if you continue to run wild around the countryside, associating with village children as if you were one of them? You mustn't forget that, now you are Sir John's stepdaughter, you have a position to maintain.'

'Are you saying that I shouldn't be friendly with Ned Fletcher any more? Is that what you mean?'

Margaret Lattimore looked uncomfortable.

'Hetty, you must realise that Ned, too, has work to do, his own life to lead. He needs to earn his keep and help his mother, he is no longer a child. You are both no longer children, to play together in idleness.'

'You never objected to Ned and me being friends together when we were poor, and lived in Mistress Fletcher's cottage,' Hetty said bitterly. 'When Papa died, you were glad enough that the Fletchers took us in and gave us a home. Are we supposed to forget them, now that you have married into money and we live in a big house and have rich relations?'

'Hetty! Of course we will never forget Mary Fletcher's kindness to us, and never miss an opportunity of helping her, now that we can return the help she gave us when we needed it. But you must realise that now I am married to Sir John, we live in different worlds from when we were poor, we move in different circles and have different obligations.'

'Does that mean we have obligations to forget our old friends, because they are not good enough for us now?' Hetty was angry, almost tearful.

She was afraid that what all this was leading up to was that Mama was going to forbid her from seeing Ned any more, and Ned was her best friend in the whole world.

'Now, Hetty, you are being ridiculous!' Margaret began to lose patience with her daughter. 'All I am saying is, that Sir John is inviting several of his friends here, and you are expected to behave in a lady-like manner while they are here, and not wander off and get into mischief with the village children. It isn't much to ask, is it, to support Sir John and help him by giving his friends a good impression of his stepdaughter?

'And Sir John is doing so much for you already, inviting eligible young men to visit us. Surely at least one among them will interest you, but with your present behaviour, I very much fear that none of them will find any attraction in you.'

'But I never said I wanted to marry!' Hetty exclaimed. 'Why can't I stay here and live at home with you? If Sir John doesn't want the burden of keeping me, I can always find work somewhere, away from Birch Hall if needs be, so that I'm not an embarrassment to him. I don't want to be married off as if I were an unwelcome burden to be disposed of to some man in need of a woman to run his household.'

'How can you say such things! You talk of Mistress Fletcher's kindness to us, and I have not, and never will, forget it, but have you not thought of the great kindness that Sir John has shown you, giving you a home and treating you as well as if you were his own flesh and blood?'

'He could as easily have suggested I stayed with Mistress Fletcher in the village,' Hetty said defiantly. 'I could have worked for my keep and been happy, as happy as we were before Sir John married you.'

The slap came suddenly, stinging her cheek and bringing tears to her eyes, tears of pain and the hurt of injustice.

'Harriet! I will not have you speak to me in that fashion! I have a mind to confine you to your room for the rest of the day for such insolence, but there is too much work to be done in preparation for the party, and everyone must help. But I shall forbid you to leave the house for the next week, and hope that by then you will have learnt some proper behaviour.

'You may not want to marry just now, but how will you feel in years to come, when you are an unwanted and unloved spinster, unmarried because your wild behaviour and ill manners has meant that no man will offer for you?'

'I'm sorry, Mama.' It wasn't a good idea to defy Mama or criticise Sir John in her hearing. Hetty had already learnt that. In the three years since her mother had married Sir John, Margaret had changed, and not, as far as Hetty could see, entirely for the better.

Hetty sighed as she prepared to follow her mother down to the kitchens to discuss with the cook and steward the arrangements for the forthcoming party. It could be much worse and she still had quite a degree of freedom.

Sir John was a kind man, and wanted nothing but good for her, that was clear. The only thing was, Hetty doubted that Sir John's wishes for her would coincide with her own.

One thing was certain, Ned wouldn't be invited to this party, or his mother. They were the two people who would have made it an enjoyable occasion for her, but as far as Hetty could see, there would be nobody except the rather pompous, elderly men whom Sir John met when he sat on the Bench at the Maidenhead Assizes, with, no doubt, their tedious and boring wives and equally tedious and boring sons or daughters.

She was not looking forward to the

party at all, though she did her duty by helping out in the kitchens and in preparing all the spare rooms for the guests, many of whom were coming from London on their way to Bath for the season, and breaking their journey to stay the night at Birch Hall.

Preparations for the party went on unceasingly for days. There was endless cooking of special, elaborate dishes and the cleaning of rooms that hadn't been used in a long time.

There was one day when Margaret and Hetty went into Maidenhead in the pony cart to make arrangements for new dresses for the occasion. To Hetty's delight, she was allowed to choose the material and a most elegant and grown-up dress was ordered from the best local seamstress. In spite of her misgivings, Hetty began to enter into the spirit of the preparations, and looked forward to the party after all.

The date had been chosen to coincide with the final gathering in of the harvest, so that workers might be spared from the fields to help in putting up seating and a large number of posts in the gardens, from which lanterns were to be hung.

There was also a great scaffolding to be erected, from which fireworks were to be let off, a popular attraction, expensive and rarely seen outside London.

Sir John's guests had to be entertained fittingly, lest they should think that people living outside London were no more than country bumpkins.

The day of the party dawned with the promise of clear skies and a mild, dry evening for the outdoor entertainments. The first guests began arriving in the middle of the afternoon. Having travelled the thirty or so miles from London they were ready to rest in their rooms until the early evening, when the local dignitaries would arrive.

Hetty was bidden to creep round the house so as not to disturb them, and later sent scurrying with pitchers of hot water, along with the maids, as soon as the travellers, fully rested, wished to wash and change into their evening finery.

So far, the guests had mostly been, as she suspected, elderly and rather dull couples, sometimes accompanied by plain, unmarried daughters who were all considerably older than Hetty and with very few interests in common with her. There were a few younger men, but still they were far too old to be of any real interest to her.

⋆　⋆　⋆

As afternoon turned to evening, the local guests began to arrive. Hetty recognised several names as Croker, Sir John's steward, announced them, but there were not many faces she knew. They came from all over the county, their carriages filling the drive and threatening to block all the lanes leading to Birch Hall.

Sir John and Hetty's mother stood in the main hall and greeted each guest as they arrived. Sir John was sporting the new fashion in waistcoats, with his coat stiffened with whalebone to make it stand out at the sides. Margaret wore a beautiful dress of gold brocade, with an overskirt of blue thread.

Both of them looked rather uncomfortable in their finery and Hetty thought it must be poor compensation to know that the cloth had come from Paris and there was no other like it in the whole of England.

Hetty herself was dressed simply, though her frock was elegant and made her look much older than her sixteen years. Margaret's personal maid had done her hair and now it was piled on her head in a complicated style which felt so insecure she didn't dare turn her head too quickly for fear of spilling hairpins and letting the whole ensemble tumble down around her shoulders.

How she wished she could be greeting Ned among the line of guests to whom she was forced to offer her hand or bow politely! Two things comforted her, though. She would see to it that Ned and Mary Fletcher had a basketful of the leftover delicacies from tonight's dinner, and Ned had promised to sneak into the grounds later that evening and watch the fireworks from the far end of the gardens. She suspected that most of the village children would have the same idea, too.

Once all the guests had arrived and been plied with liquid refreshment by the footmen and maids, the Birch Hall staff being supplemented by several hired servants brought in from Reading for the evening, Croker sounded the large gong in the hall and announced that dinner was served in the great dining hall.

He made it sound very grand, though Hetty knew that it was one of the large rooms rarely used by Sir John when only he, Margaret and Hetty were at home. Tables had been brought in, or hastily put together by local carpenters and covered with damask cloths, set out with candelabra and flower arrangements along their length.

Hetty found herself seated half way down on one side, between an elderly man who appeared to be deaf, and a daughter of one of the London guests, a girl so painfully shy she answered Hetty's attempts at conversation with almost inaudible monosyllables.

Her deaf companion ignored Hetty completely, carrying on a loud conversation with a lady across the table, who was complaining about the dreadful country roads.

'None of your London ways here, Ma'am,' he boomed. 'You're in the country now. You can't expect good roads outside the capital.'

'Well, I certainly hope there are better roads than these on the way to Bath,' the lady replied petulantly. 'I shall be shaken to pieces if I have to endure a hundred and fifty miles of the kind of roads you have in Berkshire.'

'The main road to Bath is very fair, Madam, I do assure you,' the man sitting beside her said. 'It is a good, straight road and well-maintained along its whole length.'

'But is it safe?' She found another source of concern. 'One hears such dreadful tales of highway robbery these days.' Her hand flew instinctively to her bosom and rested protectively over a large and rather ugly diamond pendant.

'Madam, the most notorious place for highwaymen is Hounslow Heath, and you are already safely past that stretch of your journey,' her companion reassured her. She was not about to abandon her fears, however, and continued to complain of the dangers of travel as if she were going on an expedition into an unexplored jungle.

Hetty listened, fascinated by the woman, who was evidently hoping that one of the gentlemen at least would offer her the protection of his company for part of the way. So far she hadn't succeeded in persuading either of them.

Hetty glanced round the table at the other guests, then looked again in surprise at the man sitting on the opposite side, some three seats down. It was the farmer, Will Foster, whom she'd met on the day of the haycart incident. He was the last person she would have expected Sir John to invite for Will, she knew, farmed a small holding a couple of miles to the south of Birch Hall and was very different from the wealthy and aristocratic guests who had come down from London.

Even the local people here tonight were all important county dignitaries, rich landowners and important towns-people from Reading and Maidenhead. As far as Hetty knew, there were no other small farmers at the party, but seeing him there, her heart lifted a little.

Here, at least, was one person among the whole company whom she felt she might be able to talk to comfortably, without the feeling of being spoken to as a child, or patronised for being a country bumpkin.

Will happened to glance in her direction at the same moment, and smiled across at her, acknowledging her with a bow. Hetty noticed he had been listening to the conversation about highwaymen with a look of quiet amusement, but now he leaned forward to address the nervous lady.

'Madam, the gentleman speaks of Hounslow Heath as being the most notorious area for highwaymen on the main road out of London, but I doubt he can have heard of our local haunt of thieves and cut-throats. Here we have Maidenhead thicket, which is infamous throughout the whole county for its highway robberies and is on our very doorstep.'

The lady gave a little scream.

'Mercy, Sir! Don't tell me I've to travel through more dangers on the road to Bath!'

'No indeed, Ma'am,' he replied seriously, his eyes on Hetty. 'You have no need to travel at all, for this house is situated in the very heart of the thicket.'

It wasn't strictly true, as the thicket did not reach quite as far as the village or Birch Hall, but there were woods surrounding the whole area which were notorious for robberies of coaches and lone horsemen. The dense undergrowth provided excellent cover for robbers and the main Bath road passed right through the thicket for a mile or more.

'Don't tell me such things!' The poor woman looked as if she might have an attack of hysterics, and Hetty, taking pity on her, said, 'Please do not fear, Ma'am. Sir John is the most important landowner hereabouts, as well as being Magistrate. No-one would dare hold up a coach carrying one of his guests, for he would know he would most certainly be hanged.'

'But what if the villain was not caught?' The lady refused to be consoled. 'And all my jewels were stolen? The diamond alone is worth a king's ransom. I would not have brought such valuables with me, but how is one to exist in Bath without such things?'

'I am sure you will be perfectly safe, Ma'am,' Hetty said. 'Several of the coaches for Bath will be leaving tomorrow together. There is always safety in numbers.' She looked across and frowned at Will. 'It was unkind of you to try to alarm us all so, Mr Foster.'

Will looked unrepentant. 'Surely it is better to be forewarned of dangers, is it not? But I do not think I could frighten you with such tales, Mistress Hetty. Someone with your fearless reputation would surely not be concerned about a mere highwayman.'

He was laughing at her! Hetty glared back at him, aware that curious glances were cast in her direction, people wondering what this reputation for fearlessness might be. The last thing she wanted was the story of her ride on the haycart to be repeated here and now, where it would become known all over the county and scandalise her mother and Sir John.

Fortunately, someone on his far side claimed Will's attention and the subject was dropped. Croker was bringing round the final course and the guests were soon too engrossed in the delicious syllabub served to them, to continue the discussion.

* ★ *

Later, as they left the dining-room to file on to the terrace to watch the fireworks, Hetty found Will beside her.

'I wonder, would one indeed ransom our German George with a bauble like the lady's pendant?' he murmured to her. 'If I were he, I'd be insulted to be ransomed for such an ugly piece.'

Hetty giggled. 'Hush, Sir! You were wicked and cruel to frighten that poor lady so with such talk!' she admonished.

'The excitement of the journey and the thought of the possibility of meeting a highwayman will help her forget the rutted roads,' he said airily. 'It will do no harm to frighten them a little. They think it is so dull in the country they are in need of a little excitement when they leave the capital.'

'I never heard anything so outrageous!' Hetty declared, but she was laughing, too. Will seemed to have the same kind of sense of fun as she herself enjoyed. Only with Ned had she felt so comfortably in tune with someone.

Will took her arm as they reached the terrace.

'Hetty,' he said earnestly, 'please do me the honour of giving me your company for the rest of the evening, for I feel like a fish out of water among all these aristocratic friends of Sir John.'

'To tell the truth, so do I,' Hetty confessed. 'I wish Sir John could have invited Ned and his mother. They'd have enjoyed the dinner so much and I'm sure the conversation would have been far livelier.'

Will chuckled. 'Yes, I think I would have felt more at home with the Fletchers than that dowager with her vulgar jewels. For tonight, though, you'll do very well instead. I'd sooner spend an evening with a lass who can climb trees and get the better of Abel

Benson than I would anyone else, even German George himself and his elegant queen.'

'You didn't tell anyone about us riding on the haycart?' Hetty asked anxiously.

'Not a word to a living soul!' Will assured her seriously. 'Though there were one or two I'd have liked to tell. One young woman in particular who would have thought it the greatest sport and would have envied you such a ride.'

'Your daughter?' Hetty asked.

Will laughed heartily. 'Nay, I'm not married. I live with my mother and my sister, Sophia. It was she who would have enjoyed the story.'

'Your sister? How old is she, then?'

'About your age, I would say.' Something in Will's manner seemed to change. He turned abruptly and said, 'Look, the fireworks are about to begin. Come to the edge of the terrace where we'll have a better view.'

Though she followed him to where a low wall afforded them a seat to view the pyrotechnics, Hetty's mind was not on the entertainment. She had few friends apart from the Fletchers and it seemed she was going to be discouraged from seeing much of them in the future. But another girl of the same age as herself would be wonderful, and Mama could hardly disapprove if Sir John had invited her brother to dine at the Hall!

It also meant that if she became friendly with Will's sister, she would have the chance to meet Will again, as well. That was beginning to seem like a very pleasurable prospect.

'Your sister,' she began, as they settled themselves on the wall. 'Do you think I might call on her one day? You see, I know so few people apart from the Fletchers and the village children and it would be — '

'My sister does not socialise much,' Will said. 'She is — she has been ill and she is still delicate. It is a nice thought but I do not think she would welcome visitors at present.'

Hetty felt as if a bowl of cold water had been thrown in her face. Will had made his sister sound as if she would be fun to know, and then made it seem as if he thought Hetty would be a bad influence on the girl.

Hetty was silent, nursing her hurt. She watched the fireworks and wondered if Ned was also watching them too, from the far end of the grounds. She hoped he was enjoying them but for herself they passed in a dazzle of bright lights. She was too busy thinking.

What was there to stop her calling on Mrs Foster, a social visit from one neighbour to another, since she had now met Will socially? If his sister really was too delicate and ill for visitors, she would find out for herself. If Mrs Foster was welcoming, then Will could hardly stop her making friends with his sister.

Something in the way he had spoken intrigued Hetty. What really was the reason Will didn't want her to meet his sister? Hetty was determined to find out.

3

It was late when the coaches for the local people were brought to the front door, along with the horses for the gentlemen who had ridden over from nearby villages and estates. Will had been by Hetty's side through most of the evening, proving good and entertaining company.

She decided it was better not to mention his sister again, since he seemed so reluctant to encourage Hetty to visit, so reluctant even to talk about her. In spite of this, by the time Will's horse was brought from the stables, she felt she knew him quite well, and liked what she knew.

Neither of them knew any of the other guests, except a few by name, and this had given them an added incentive to stay in each other's company.

When it was time for him to leave,

Hetty followed him out on to the drive to see him mount his horse, hoping that he might suggest at least that she called on his mother socially. She didn't dare suggest it, in case he discouraged her again, but she was determined in her own mind that she would find some excuse to visit the Foster farm before too long.

The guests who had come from London were slow to leave next morning. A few of them, anxious to travel on towards Bristol or Bath, left after breakfast so that they could make as good progress as possible in daylight and reach Hungerford or even Marlborough before dusk, but others, including the lady who had been teased and frightened at dinner, elected to stay on a day more.

Hetty learned her name was Lady Mountjoy, a rich widow who spent most of her time entertaining at her London mansion, but who had been persuaded that the London fogs were not good for her health and that she should spend the winter in the improved air of the country.

The idea of shutting herself away from all entertainments and pleasures of the capital for months on end, held nothing but horror for the lady, but having been told that Bath was at least as lively as London and half her acquaintances would be there, she had decided to brave the dangers and perils of travel and see for herself.

She was a very nervous traveller, but the thought of travelling in the company of others had encouraged her, and Sir John had promised that he would provide an armed escort of his own men to see the coaches safely through the thicket and on their way.

* * *

Hetty spent much of the morning after the party, helping to entertain those still remaining, and found it rather hard going. By afternoon, she was becoming very tired of making small talk with

51

ladies she did not know, and did not particularly wish to know, or parrying well-meant teasing from gentlemen who asked her, with boring repetition, if there were soon to be an announcement of a betrothal, and if Sir John would be giving another party in her honour soon.

When Mama was busily engaged in taking tea with some of the ladies, she slipped upstairs, changed out of her smart clothes into a riding habit, and stole out of the side door, making towards the stables.

Her special pony, Firefly, greeted her and nuzzled her hand as she reached to stroke him. Thomas, one of the grooms, was cleaning tackle and she asked him to saddle the pony for her.

He looked doubtful. 'Sir John would not want you to ride out by yourself, Miss Hetty.'

'I'm not going far. Sir John won't mind my going alone. Heavens, I know all the byways better than he does, I expect. I've lived here all my life! And you have far too much to do here. What if one of the guest wishes his horse brought round, and you are not available to do it?'

'That's true.' Thomas looked relieved and went to fetch Firefly's saddle. He knew Miss Hetty was a good horse-woman and there was no reason for her to come to harm in daylight.

'You'd best be back before dusk,' he warned, as she led the pony out of the stables. 'Sir John will be angered if harm comes to you, and I haven't been with you.'

'Sir John won't even know I've been out riding,' Hetty said truthfully. 'He's far too busy entertaining his guests to be bothered with such matters.'

She had really only planned to ride down to the village to see Mary Fletcher and Ned, but when Hetty reached their cottage there was no-one about, the place shut and empty.

Unwilling to ride back to Birch Hall so soon and have to listen to Sir John's guests discussing the latest French fashions or twitting to her about a possible betrothal, Hetty rode on, out of the village and along a lane that ran between fields towards a small wood.

It wasn't long before she realised that she had never been as far as this before. When she had lived with the Fletchers in the village there had been no question of riding anywhere, and so her knowledge of the countryside was bounded by the distance she could walk.

A feeling of adventurousness came over her unexpectedly, and, turning Firefly towards a gap in the hedge, she left the road and began to urge him into a canter across the field, towards the woods.

It was exhilarating, to feel the wind on her face, her hair falling from its restraining pins and flying out behind her. She urged Firefly on. She had never ridden him as fast as this before, and she could feel the pony responding, sensing the freedom he had never known before.

Less than a dozen yards from the edge of the wood, disaster struck. It could have been a rabbit hole, or maybe a tree root. Firefly tripped, broke his stride and stumbled, flinging Hetty from the saddle and sending her thudding on to the ground.

For a moment she lay there, winded. As she recovered she saw that she had landed on a fat tussock of grass which had broken her fall. Cautiously she sat up and moved each arm and leg, finding to her surprise and relief she had not broken anything.

She scrambled to her feet and looked around for Firefly. He was a short distance away, just inside the wood, cropping grass unconcernedly, but when she walked towards him he edged away and she saw that he was limping.

Clearly, she couldn't ride him if he was lame and she wondered what on earth she was going to do. She wasn't entirely sure where she was, except that it was some distance from Birch Hall and there seemed no-one around and no cottage in sight where she could call and ask for help.

She followed Firefly into the wood, where he paused at the edge of a clearing and began cropping again. Hetty sat down on a fallen log as near to him as he seemed disposed to let her, and tried to think what to do.

When she looked over at him, it seemed to her that the pony's leg had become swollen, already it appeared noticeable.

Hetty supposed that the only thing to do would be to tether him here and go back to the village for help. The blacksmith, she thought, would be the best person to speak to, for the last people she wanted to involve were the grooms at Birch Hall.

They would tell Sir John and he and Mama would never let her ride out unaccompanied again. The trouble was, if she left Firefly it was likely he'd be stolen before she could return.

While she sat thinking what to do, Hetty heard a rustling sound from the far side of the clearing. Expecting to see a fawn, she kept perfectly still and after a moment, to her surprise, a small gypsy girl came into the clearing, black haired, skin brown as a nut and her skirt and blouse dirty and ragged. Her eyes were on Firefly and at first she didn't notice Hetty.

She moved noiselessly towards the pony but when she was nearly touching him he shied suddenly and moved away. Looking up, the girl saw Hetty.

'He yours?' she asked.

'Yes. He tripped and now he's lame. I don't know what to do,' Hetty replied, feeling foolish.

The girl crept up to Firefly from behind, moving cautiously and muttering to herself, or perhaps she was reassuring her pony, for he turned his head and snorted, then went back to cropping the grass without moving.

She took the bridle and began stroking his head and mane, still muttering in a strange language.

When she had calmed Firefly, she

slid her hand down over the injured leg. He flinched, but did not shy away this time.

After she had run her hand over his leg, the gypsy girl nodded, as if confirming something she had suspected. She looked across at Hetty.

'He pulled a muscle,' she said. 'Nothing too serious. A poultice of comfrey will cure it.'

'Comfrey?' Hetty said blankly.

The girl regarded her pityingly. 'My people are horse dealers. We know about these things. You want I should heal him for you?'

'Oh, would you? I'm miles from home and I don't know what to do,' Hetty replied eagerly.

'Help me search for comfrey leaves,' the girl said. 'We need a big bunch.'

'What do they look like?' Hetty asked.

The girl looked at her as if she thought Hetty was particularly stupid and quietly said, 'I'll fetch some,' and disappeared into the undergrowth at the other side of the clearing, making no sound whatsoever.

Hetty stayed sitting on the log, watching Firefly and wondering if the girl could really cure him. Of course, she might return with several men from her tribe and steal him, together with anything else of value they could find. Hetty had never met a gypsy before, and knew little about them except the rumours and tales she had heard from the villagers, who all mistrusted them.

She had almost convinced herself to run off before something worse happened, when the girl reappeared as silently as she'd gone, this time carrying an armful of green plants. With barely a glance at Hetty, she dropped to her knees by the pony and began wrapping the leaves round the injured leg, binding them in place with strips of rush.

All the while she was muttering to herself in a strange tongue. Hetty watched, fascinated and impressed by the way Firefly kept still and allowed her to do as she wanted. He seemed to understand that it was for his benefit, and even moved his foot a little to make it easier for her to reach round it.

'Do now,' the gypsy girl said, when all the comfrey leaves had been securely wrapped round Firefly's leg. 'Now we leave him until sun sinks below those far trees.' She pointed across the field towards the autumn sun, already low in the sky. 'Then, he be well enough to lead back. Not ride, give him two days with the comfrey close against his leg. After that, he will be well.'

'How did you learn to treat horses?' Hetty asked.

'I told you. My people are horse traders. Not horse thieves. We are honest folk, but Romanies are not trusted here.'

'I trust you,' Hetty said impulsively. She liked the girl, who looked little more than a child, but her face was old and wise looking, making it impossible to guess at her age.

'What's your name?'

'You can call me Meg.' The way she

said it made Hetty wonder if it was her real name or merely the name she gave when asked. Perhaps she had another name she used within her tribe.

She came to sit beside Hetty on the log, but did not take her eyes from the pony, who now cropped contentedly at the far edge of the clearing, seeming unconcerned by the leaves stepped to his leg.

'I've no money on me to give you for what you've done,' Hetty said, 'but will you take this? It's all I have.' She unfastened a gold chain she wore round her neck, holding it out to Meg.

To her surprise, the girl shrank back, looking fearful, and shook her head.

'Nay, 'tis too much. They will say I stole it.' She pushed Hetty's hand away. 'I like the beasts, I cannot abide to see one discomforted. I did it for him, not you.'

'Thank you. But I wish I could show you how grateful I am. I don't know what I would have done if you hadn't come along,' Hetty said awkwardly.

'I will read your palm while we wait for the comfrey to do its work,' Meg said suddenly, taking Hetty's hand in her own small, calloused one. She peered at it closely, then took Hetty's other hand and compared the palms. Hetty watched her eyes widen in surprise. 'This is not what I was expecting,' Meg said. 'This is very strange.'

'What is?' Hetty knew a moment of excitement. Was she going to have a very different life from the rather dull and uneventful one that she had always imagined lay before her? She didn't know whether she really believed in fortune telling, but at this moment she wanted to believe that something different and exciting would happen to her.

'You will have a happy life in front of you. A happy marriage and be blessed with children,' Meg intoned flatly. She sounded as if she said such things to everyone whose palm she read. Hetty was sure the girl had seen much more.

'What else did you see?' she demanded. 'You said it wasn't what you expected. A happy marriage and children is what everyone expects.'

Meg looked away. Then she looked into Hetty's face and said, 'But it is true. You will be happy and be blessed with children. But not yet. First, I see danger, and much trouble. And I see more. There are great riches that you will hold in your hand — diamonds and rubies and gold — much of value. But not for you. You will never own them, you must never keep them or you will rue the day. You will not be poor, but neither will you have the riches that seem to be there for the taking.'

'Whatever do you mean?'

The gypsy girl folded Hetty's fingers over her palms and gently pushed the hands away.

'I see no more,' she said. 'I do not know what it means but it is all there, written for those with the knowledge to read.'

She stood up and walked over to

Firefly, talking to him softly in her strange language. He was not normally good with strangers, but he nuzzled Meg and made no resistance when she bent to feel his leg under the pad of comfrey. Meg looked back over her shoulder at the sinking sun, then came back to Hetty.

'You can take him now,' she said. 'Don't try to ride him. Walk him back slow and if he wants to stop a while, then you stop, too. Go at his pace and he will not damage his leg. He is a wise horse and I have told him what to do. Keep the comfrey on until tomorrow and the swelling should be gone by then.'

'Thank you, Meg.'

The words seemed inadequate for the gratitude Hetty felt and she wished she could offer the girl something.

Meg seemed to know this, and said, 'Now, you tell your people not all Romany folk are thieves. But I think you will not want to tell how you came to be here and lamed your beast.'

64

Meg was a little too perceptive for comfort, Hetty thought. She would have a great deal of explaining to do when she reached Birch Hall, for at the pace she'd have to go it would be completely dark before she returned and no doubt both Sir John and Mama would be furious. They might even have some of the estate workers out looking for her already.

'Farewell. Go safely, but remember, there will be much danger for you ahead,' Meg said. Before Hetty had even picked up Firefly's leading rein, she had disappeared into the gathering gloom of the forest.

It was a long, slow journey back to Birch Hall. Firefly ambled slowly along the lanes, stopping to crop the grass after every few yards, and Hetty herself needed to rest from time to time. It was the farthest she had ever walked and now it was quite dark, only the hard surface of the lane under her feet to tell her she was still going in the right direction.

Later, there would be a moon but it had not yet risen and it was not until she saw the lights from the cottages in the village that she was completely sure where she was, and that there was not much farther to go.

She should be thinking of what she was going to say to explain her absence for so long, and the fact that she had gone out without a groom to escort her in the first place. She couldn't explain about Firefly's lameness without mentioning Meg, and she knew that Sir John disliked gypsies very strongly.

Whenever they came before him at the Magistrates' Court or the Assizes, he tended to assume guilt because of who they were, and their lifestyle. Hetty wondered if it would ever be possible to persuade him that not all of the Romany people were dishonest. She owed it to Meg in gratitude to try, at least.

Meg had shown she was honest by refusing the gold chain when she could have sold it easily in another town, and what she had done to help was surely worth that much.

Hetty had still not thought up a plausible excuse by the time she pushed open the gates of Birch Hall and led Firefly up the drive. She took him straight round the side of the house to the stables, which were in darkness. She lit a candle and began unsaddling him and was bringing water to his stall when a sleepy-eyed stable boy appeared from the hayloft above, where he had been sleeping.

'Mistress Hetty!' he said in surprise. 'What has happened to you? I thought you must be staying overnight when you did not return by nightfall.'

'Firefly tripped and sprained a muscle. I had to walk him home,' Hetty explained, trying to sound casual.

'What's this all round his leg?' The boy was prodding at the comfrey and Firefly jerked back irritably.

'Comfrey,' Hetty said. 'It's very good for healing swelling on a horse's leg. And other things too, I believe. Did you not know that?'

'Ay,' the boy said. 'I've heard tell o' comfrey but I've not used it meself. How come you knew to wrap his leg in it?' He peered at Firefly's leg, holding the candle close to see it better. 'And so neatly fastened, too.'

'Leave it on until tomorrow. Then, you can take it off if the swelling has gone down, but don't walk him for a day more.'

'Eh, but you sound like a real horse doctor. Where did you learn such skills?' He straightened up, staring curiously at Hetty.

'I thought everyone knew about the healing skills of comfrey,' Hetty said airily. Plainly the lad didn't. When he saw how effective the herb was, he would think her the county's expert on horse medicine.

Or a witch.

Hetty slipped back into the house through a side door. She would have liked to have gone up to her room at once, but Mama would be waiting for her, either in the salon or in her own room and Hetty knew she would have to face her as soon as possible and explain as best she could.

Crossing the main hall she met Sir John's steward, coming out of the drawing-room with a tray.

'Croker, where is Mama?' she asked. If both her mother and Sir John were waiting in the drawing-room for her, it looked as if they were really very angry and she was in for a serious punishment.

'Why, in the drawing-room with Sir John, trying to pacify the poor lady,' Croker said. 'Did you not know? Have you not heard what happened this afternoon?'

'No, I — I've been out since after lunch. What is wrong?' Hetty asked, anxiously.

'Lady Mountjoy's coach has been held up by a highwayman, and she has been robbed of all her jewels,' Croker said. 'The poor lady has been beside herself ever since. The Master and Mistress have done their best but she has been hysterical and they have had to send for Dr Walton.'

'A highwayman!' Hetty gasped. 'How on earth could that have happened? She was travelling with several others, and in daylight!'

'It would seem that was not the case,' Croker told her. 'You had best ask Sir John or Lady Lattimore if you want to know more. They have been with her ever since Lady Mountjoy returned, before dusk.'

'Was Mama looking for me?' Hetty asked.

'Her Ladyship has not spoken to me about you. I would think Her Ladyship has had more important things to concern her at present.' Croker dropped his voice to say confidentially, 'If I were you, Miss, I would change out of my outdoor clothes before coming into the drawing-room. They will not want to know you were away from home while a dastardly cut-throat has been roaming the area.'

'Thank you, Croker.' Hetty ran

upstairs and changed into a gown suitable for evening, before coming back and entering the drawing-room.

Margaret Lattimore barely acknowledged her daughter's presence. She was holding a bunch of burnt feathers under Lady Mountjoy's nose in an attempt to revive her from a faint. The lady was stretched out on a chaise longue and emitting little shrieks from time to time. As Hetty drew near, she sat up and clasped her by the hand.

'Oh, Hetty, it was terrible! The nightmare I have gone through!' Here was a new audience to whom to tell her tale. 'Robbed! Held up at pistol point by an evil man! He was a monster! A man all in black with a tricorn hat and cloak, and with a mask over his face!'

'But how could this have happened, Mama?' Hetty asked. 'I thought Lady Mountjoy was leaving to travel with several of the other coaches and horsemen, and in daylight? How could she be robbed, with so many others to protect her?'

'That was the arrangement, but there was delay.' Margaret dropped her voice and whispered, 'Lady Mountjoy took so long in attiring herself ready for the journey that I fear the others left without her. I think they may have assumed she was staying a further night here.

'When she eventually left, she ordered her coachman to catch the others up, and they might well have done, but by then Lady Mountjoy's coach was separated from the others by a goodly distance and driving alone through our notorious thicket.'

Lady Mountjoy was becoming hysterical again.

'I should never have attempted Bath. I should have returned to London. But then, there was Hounslow Heath to traverse again and where am I to go in London when all my acquaintances are enjoying the season in the West Country and London is so dull at present? That man at dinner last night. He knew, he warned me,' she babbled.

'He said the thicket was the most dangerous place to travel.'

'Who is this man she keeps talking about?' Margaret asked. 'Hetty, do you know? She says he warned her about highwaymen in our thicket and frightened her with tales of robbers during dinner. Surely, Sir John did not invite a highwayman himself to our party?'

Hetty remembered Will Foster's teasing. But surely, he could not have been planning a highway robbery?

'The gentlemen were merely discussing the route between London and Bath, and saying that the travellers had already passed the most dangerous stretch of the road. Our Maidenhead thicket was mentioned, but only in passing,' Hetty replied.

'Who were these people sitting near her, then?' Margaret demanded. 'It sounds as though they might have known something more than most, to talk in that way. Do you know who they were, Hetty?'

'It was — ' Hetty pulled herself up.

'It was someone who was a friend of Sir John, Mama,' she said. 'I didn't really know him. I don't think I knew anyone at the dinner table last night.'

'Probably just idle talk, Sir John broke in. He had been standing by the window at the far end of the room. Women's emotions were not something he understood or could cope with, and he had kept well out of the way while his wife ministered to Lady Mountjoy.

'Madam,' he addressed her. 'When you are feeling well enough to travel, whether it is on to Bath or to return to London, I shall personally provide an armed escort for you and see that you are safely delivered to your chosen destination.'

Lady Mountjoy was not to be mollified. 'And what good will that be, now that all my valuables are gone? They might as well hold up my coach and shoot me, for my old bones are all that is left for them to steal now.'

'You may be sure that all my constables are out searching for the villain,' Sir John assured her. 'We shall find him, never fear, and then he will go for trial and I shall have the satisfaction of sending him to the gallows.'

'And will that bring back my pendant?' Lady Mountjoy cried. 'Given to me by my late husband and worth a king's ransom! Not to mention my rings, my brooches, everything I had with me, along with all the money I was carrying!'

'Rest assured, already my men are working to recover your goods,' Sir John said soothingly. Hetty hardly heard him, she was remembering that phrase, 'worth a king's ransom', and Will's mocking remark about whether King George would be insulted to think he might be ransomed with such an ugly jewel.

Surely, Will could not have planned to steal it! And if he had, he would hardly have spoken in such a way as to put the lady on her guard? But perhaps he knew that it was likely that there would be robbers abroad that night, and he was deliberately warning Lady Mountjoy? If so, how did he know?

There was certainly more to Will Foster than she had at first thought, and it made Hetty all the more determined to get to know him better. The way to do that would be to meet his family, and she planned to visit his mother and sister as soon as she possibly could.

4

It was two days later before Hetty was able to carry out her plan to visit Will Foster's farm and introduce herself to his mother and sister. By then, Lady Mountjoy had been persuaded to continue her journey to Bath, accompanied at great inconvenience and expense to Sir John, by several of his workforce.

They took her as far as Reading, where she could continue under the escort of the mail coach, which always travelled with armed guards.

'I trust that's the last we'll hear of her,' Sir John said, when his men, having lost nearly three days' work, returned to report to him.

'Not, I fear, if you do not manage to catch the man responsible, and recover her jewels,' Margaret said. 'She will expect nothing less from you and I suspect we shall hear from her by every post, enquiring about both.'

Sir John sighed. 'God knows I am as determined to root out these villains as anyone. I shall issue a reward for information. That might induce some of the criminal fraternity to turn King's Evidence, especially if they are promised a free pardon for any lesser misdemeanours.'

As soon as she could, Hetty went to the stables to see how Firefly was recovering.

'The swelling has quite gone, Miss Hetty,' Thomas told her. 'He couldn't have been as badly hurt as you thought, for it to improve so quickly.'

Hetty knew perfectly well that Firefly had sustained a bad sprain, but she wasn't about to argue with the stable boy. If too much was made of the pony's quick recovery she would be drawn into telling too many details of how Firefly came to be cured so quickly.

Firefly having been pronounced fit to ride again, Hetty ordered him to be saddled at once.

'You want me to come with you?' Thomas was clearly not enthusiastic. With most of the workers having been away escorting Lady Mountjoy, there was extra work for those staying at home.

'No, I'm not going far. And I'll be safe. I don't look worth robbing.' Hetty joked.

Thomas looked doubtful. ' 'Tis no joke, Miss Hetty. You best keep well clear of the thicket, even in daylight. Robbers are no respecters of persons.'

'I'm not going anywhere near the thicket,' Hetty assured him. 'I'm visiting a friend just a mile or so away and I've told Mama where I shall be.'

Reluctantly, Thomas let Hetty mount and ride off down the drive. Will's farm lay to the south, across the main Bath road, near the village of Charvil. Hetty knew how to reach the village and enquiries of one of the locals directed her to Will Foster's farm.

As she approached down a narrow

lane, she looked at the building curiously. It was a low lying, thatched farmhouse, but there had been extensions added to it from time to time.

In front of the house hens and geese ran freely, and there was a farmyard away to one side. Directly in front of the house was a garden, the flowerbeds neatly kept and full of autumn blooms.

Hetty tethered Firefly to a tree just inside the gate, and walked down the path to the front door. She knocked, but while she waited she started to have doubts as to whether she had been too bold or presumptious in visiting uninvited.

For a long time nothing happened, then, just as Hetty was deciding whether to knock again, the door opened a few inches and an untidy looking servant girl peered out at her.

'Yessum?' She looked wary.

'I'm Hetty Neville, from Birch Hall. I've come to pay a social call on Mistress Foster. Would you please see if she would be kind enough to receive me?'

The girl disappeared, shutting the door and leaving Hetty still standing outside. She heard footsteps retreating inside, and then what sounded like a whispered conversation.

Finally, there were more footsteps, brisker this time, and the door was tugged open wider with some difficulty. It seemed the front door was not much used by the family.

A plump, middle-aged woman in a blue frock covered with a large apron, stood in the doorway. She had a look of Will about her.

'Mistress Neville! You honour us by a visit, but we did not expect — Will said he had spoken to you at length at Sir John's reception, but I did not think — oh, please do come in!'

The poor woman was plainly flustered but she stepped back and ushered Hetty inside, leading her into a small room to the left of the hallway. It was full of heavy furniture, smelt damp and cold and was clearly the best parlour, rarely used.

'I'll get Jane to light the fire,' Mistress Foster said. 'Please sit down, Mistress Neville. May I offer you a dish of tea?'

Hetty was consumed with embarrassment. This formality was not at all what she had expected or wanted.

'My name is Hetty.' She smiled at her hostess. 'Mama and I used to live in a house like this in Burchetts Green when I was a child, before she married Sir John. I remember how we all used to sit in the kitchen, the cosiest room in the house.

'If you have no objection, I would much prefer to sit in the kitchen and talk to you.'

'Of course, my dear, if that is really what you'd prefer.' Mistress Foster looked relieved. 'I'm afraid this house is not what you are used to.'

'Neither is Birch Hall,' Hetty said firmly. She followed Mistress Foster down the passage into another room at the back of the farmhouse. Here she felt far more at home. Here were all the sights, sounds and smells that immediately brought to mind Mary Fletcher's cottage.

Mistress Foster pulled up a rocking-chair and invited Hetty to sit down. She poured some home-brewed ale from a jug and placed a mug of it, with a plate of saffron cakes, on the table beside her.

'Will told me all about the grand reception and dinner Sir John gave,' she said, seating herself on a wooden chair opposite. 'So many important people down from London, and all our county dignitaries there, too. It must have been a wonderful sight to see them in all their finery.'

'I hardly knew anyone there,' Hetty confessed. 'They were all Sir John's friends either from London or country people whom we did not know. That's why I was so glad when I saw Mr Foster near me at the table. I met him when I was with Ned Fletcher, a few days before.'

'Aye, our Will said as he'd seen you

there, and he was glad of your presence, too, for he didn't know anyone either.' Mistress Foster smiled at Hetty. 'He's away from the farm at present, or he'd be pleased to welcome you himself. We hardly ever have visitors, so you must forgive me if I appear unused to company.'

'I have no visitors of my own at Birch Hall,' Hetty said. 'Everyone who comes is someone for Sir John. Even Mama rarely has any friends visit. The ones we knew when we were poor and lived with Mary Fletcher wouldn't feel easy about coming now, and we have lost touch with most of those we knew before Mama was widowed.'

Mistress Foster glanced out of the window, then sprang to her feet.

'Lord save us! The pigs have got into the front garden again! You must excuse me, my dear, but I must run and shoo them out! Stay and have your cake. I'll not be long.' She hurried out of the back door leading to the yard and after a moment Hetty saw her pass the window, shouting and waving her arms.

A moment later, the door opposite from the passage, burst open and a girl about Hetty's age came running in.

'Mama! Who was that at the door? I thought — Oh!' She stopped short at the sight of Hetty, and her hands flew up to cover her face. She seemed terrified.

'It was I at the door,' Hetty said. 'I came to visit. Are you Sophia?'

To her astonishment, the girl shrank back against the wall. She still had her hands over her face.

'What's wrong?' Hetty asked. 'Surely you're not frightened of me? I'm Hetty Neville, from Birch Hall. Do I really look such a monster?'

The girl shook her head, then muttered through her fingers something Hetty did not catch.

'What did you say?' Hetty asked.

'You're not a monster. I am,' she said.

Hetty stood up and came nearer. 'Whatever do you mean? Why are you hiding yourself like that?'

'I can't be seen. I'm too ugly,' the girl whispered.

'Ugly? How can you be ugly? You have the prettiest hair I've ever seen and — ' Hetty peered at her and saw the girl's eyes fixed on her ' — you have the most beautiful eyes. Who says you're ugly? Who could be so cruel as to say such a thing to you?'

'It's true.' There was a catch in the girl's voice. 'You mustn't see my face. No-one must. I had the smallpox when I was a child and it destroyed my face.'

'And no-one has been allowed to see you since?' Hetty was beginning to understand why Will had been so reluctant to let anyone visit, and why Mistress Foster had said they rarely had visitors.

'Aren't you very lonely, seeing no-one?' she asked.

Sophia nodded.

'I'm lonely too,' Hetty said. 'That's why I came to visit, when your brother said he had a sister about my age. I hoped we might be friends. And, you know, friends aren't concerned with looks. It's what people are like inside that matters. I do hope we can be friends, but I don't see how that can be if I'm never to see you.'

Sophia came a step nearer.

'But I look — ' she whispered, her hands still in front of her face.

'What do you think when you look in the mirror? Really look?' Hetty asked.

Sophia shook her head. 'I never look. I never have,' she said. 'I couldn't.'

'Then how can you possibly know that you're ugly? You couldn't be, with such hair and those lovely eyes!'

'Have I really? Lovely eyes, I mean?' She sounded surprised.

'Yes, what I can see of them. Please, let us be friends. I'd so like that.'

'I would, too.' There was a world of longing in the words.

'Then let me meet you properly. I promise I won't scream, or faint.' Hetty wished she hadn't been so facetious when Sophia shrank back again, shaking her head.

Hetty reached out and gently took hold of one hand, easing the fingers away. Reluctantly, first one hand, then the other, dropped from Sophia's face.

She turned to face Hetty and said, defiantly, 'There! Now you know! And if you want to go home now, I wouldn't blame you. You couldn't want a friend who looks like I do.'

Hetty stared at Sophia for a long moment. The skin of her face was pock-marked badly, but over the years what must have been terrible scarring, had faded considerably. Her bone structure was still good and Hetty realised that, if it hadn't been for the disease, Sophia would have been an exceptionally beautiful girl.

'And the last time you looked in the mirror was when you first had the smallpox?' she said gently.

'Yes. And never since. I couldn't bear to.' The large brown eyes filled with tears. 'Oh, Hetty, I wish I was like other girls!'

'There are lots of other girls who had the pox when they were young. But over the years the scarring faded, like yours has. The marks are still there, but not nearly as bad as it must have been when you first had the disease. Has no-one told you to look and see the improvement?'

'That's what I've told her, time and again.' Mistress Foster came in from the back door and saw the two girls, facing each other. 'At last here's someone who'll tell you the truth and make you believe it. Miss Hetty, your coming here has been the best thing that's happened for years.'

'And am I really? You can honestly tell me that you can look at my face and not be disgusted by it?' Sophia looked dazed.

'Yes. Let's be friends. Say you want us to be.' Hetty put her hands on Sophia's shoulders and kissed her cheeks. The skin felt rough under her lips and she had the feeling that Sophia had not been kissed on her face since her illness.

When she turned to Mistress Foster, she saw tears streaming down the older woman's face.

'Bless you, my dear,' she whispered.

Hetty stayed as long as she could, and promised to come again very soon. Once over her initial inhibitions, Sophia proved good company and a delightful and interesting person to know. She had been accustomed to taking long solitary walks in the surrounding countryside, and promised to show Hetty the haunts of wildlife and where rare flowers grew in the local woods.

'Come again, come often now,' she said. 'You've seen me as I truly am, and accepted me, but I'm not sure about other people. I couldn't go into the village. I'd be afraid of everyone staring at me.'

'They'd stare because they hadn't seen you before,' Hetty said. 'Like they might stare at me if I went somewhere new. Get used to not hiding your face, and get used to seeing what you really look like, first. Then, we'll see what the rest of the world makes of us both.'

When Hetty left for home, Sophia walked with her to where Firefly, tethered to a tree by the gate, was placidly cropping grass.

'Nice pony.' Sophia stroked his velvety muzzle and pressed her face against his nose. Firefly whinnied softly and Hetty was reminded for an instant of Meg, the gypsy girl.

'You have an affinity with horses,' Hetty said.

'Yes, all animals. They have never minded what I look like.' Sophia stepped back and gave Firefly an appraising look, the look of an expert. 'Our farm horses are just for work, not as pretty as your pony, but, I have to say, yours is not as fine as the black horse.'

'What black horse?' Hetty asked.

'Ah! He's a secret horse. I came upon him by chance a while back. I will show you next time you come.'

'A secret horse?' Hetty was intrigued.

'Yes. But I will say nothing now. That will ensure you come back to visit us again soon.' She watched Hetty mount and trot off down the lane.

★ ★ ★

They were at dinner that evening when Croker came with a message for Sir John. It had to be very important for him to have interrupted the meal and at first Sir John looked annoyed, then, as Croker spoke in a low tone, he rose from the table, saying, 'Margaret, my dear, I apologise for disturbing your table, but Croker has brought distressing news which calls for my immediate attention.

'It seems that our notorious robbers have been active again, in spite of all the efforts of the local enforcement officers. The mail coach from London has been held up and robbed this very evening, in the heart of the thicket, not far from the very place where Lady Mountjoy was attacked.'

Margaret gasped. 'The same man!' she whispered.

'Until we catch him, we won't know if this is the work of the same man alone, or a gang working together,' Sir John said grimly. 'I shall order the notices asking for information to be posted everywhere, and double the reward for capture. If he is so cunning he eludes all those hunting for him, perhaps the inducement of money will persuade one of his fellows to turn the King's Evidence against him.'

The whole village was talking about the mail coach robbery the next day. It seemed that there had been two men involved, or a man and a boy, perhaps, since one of the robbers appeared to be smaller than the other, though both were masked and armed with pistols, looking equally fierce.

In spite of the coachman being armed, he was forced at pistol point to stop and dismount, together with the two guards who rode at the rear of the coach. They were tied up before they could reach for their blunderbusses, which were more for intimidation than use, being cumbersome and slow to load and fire. One of the robbers cut the traces of the coach and set the horses galloping off into the night, then both men had taken the smaller bags which contained valuables, tossing those they couldn't carry into the bushes, either to an accomplice or to be collected later.

The larger bags, containing mail, they had ignored. They had then ridden off, leaving the coachman and his colleagues tied up and the coach, horseless, straddling the road. It was not until an hour later, when a lone horseman passed by, that the men were rescued. By then, of course, there was no trace of the highwaymen.

'They clearly knew their business,' the coachman, interviewed by Sir John, said. He was ashamed of the humiliation of being held up and robbed, but anxious to justify himself. 'We could do nothing. It all happened so quickly. The first man rose out of the bushes right in front of us. I had to rein in, else I would have run him down. Wish that I had, now, except that our poor horses would have suffered.'

'Why did you not have pistols on board, and have them primed and at the ready?' Sir John demanded.

'Your Lordship, we weren't carrying passengers and the cargo was mostly mail. We did not think we were a rich enough target for highway robbery. There were pistols on board, in the lockers, but we had come safely through Hounslow Heath and it seemed that the road was open and safe until we passed Newbury and entered the open downland.'

'But you did have valuables on board,' Sir John insisted. 'I have information from London that there were goods from a famous jeweller being sent to Bristol, for shipment abroad, as well as a large quantity of gold; payment for goods arriving by boat at that port.

'This is gross negligence of duty and I shall have you all arrested. How am I to know that you were not in league with these highwaymen yourselves, to allow them to overpower you so easily?'

To Margaret, later, he said, 'I do not think the crew of the mail coach were in any way involved, but a time in the jailhouse may go some way to sharpen their wits and help them remember a more detailed description of these highway robbers. By Heaven, Margaret, our locality is becoming notorious for highwaymen, and I shall not rest until this evil is stopped!

'Sir George Astley, a fellow magistrate, is coming here shortly to discuss plans with me. I think, between us, we will catch these crooks and if we act quickly enough, mayhap we will also recover some of their spoils.'

5

Hetty was impatient to see her new friend, Sophia, again, but it was several days before she was able to set out for Foster's farm. At last, there came a morning when Margaret was busy discussing some planned new dresses with her maid, Hawkins, and Hetty was able to slip out to the stables and order Thomas to saddle Firefly for her.

He was used by now to her riding out alone, and did not suggest he come with her. As soon as she was out of the gates of Birch Hall, she turned her pony towards the village of Charvil and trotted along the lanes to Foster's farm.

She was crossing the yard in front of the house, having tethered Firefly by the gate as usual, when someone came out of a barn nearby, carrying a bucket and a hoe.

'Ned! What on earth are you doing here?' It was some time since Hetty had last seen Ned. She guessed that he must by now have found work somewhere, but it never occurred to her that it might be here.

'Been working for Will for some time now,' Ned said. 'It's good, here. Will's a good master and Mistress Foster feeds me well.'

'I'm glad you've found a good place, Ned. It will be a great help to your mother to know you've a steady job as a farm worker.'

Ned gave her an odd, sideways look. 'I'm more'n a farm worker, Hetty. Reckon I could end up much more important than a farm worker.'

'Own your own farm one day, perhaps?' Hetty smiled at him. The likelihood of Ned ever having a farm of his own was very remote, but she couldn't crush his dreams.

'Nay, not as a farmer. Maybe better even than that.' He shuffled off towards the fields at the back of the farm, looking as if he thought he might have said too much.

Hetty turned away, glad to have seen Ned but hoping he wasn't raising his ambitions impossibly high. She had barely gone a dozen paces farther when Will came round the side of the building, and hailed her.

'Mistress Hetty! I'm so pleased you have come back again! You have no idea how much your last visit meant to my sister. It has done so much for her, it has changed her life, indeed it has.'

Hetty smiled shyly. 'I thought that maybe you didn't want me to come visiting when you first spoke of your sister. I came at first partly because you sounded discouraging, and when I met Sophia I understood why. But it's such a shame that she should hide herself away because she thought she had a worse affliction than she has. She is still a very lovely girl.'

'Aye, she was a beautiful child. And she still is, if she can ever bring herself to believe it. My mother and I can never thank you enough for giving her confidence in herself.'

'I'm just happy to have found a new friend,' Hetty said modestly. 'Is Sophia at home?'

Will laughed. 'Sophia is always at home. Well, not when she is wandering around the fields by herself, but she never goes far, not off our land, anyway.' Then he added, 'But perhaps that will not always be true, now that she has found you. Go and find her in the kitchen with my mother. She will be so delighted that you have come to visit again.'

Hetty went round to the back of the farmhouse and knocked on the back door. She could hear Sophia's light footsteps running to answer her knock.

'You must share our meal today,' Sophia said eagerly, dancing from one foot to the other with excitement. 'And then I will take you to see all over the farm.'

Will came in to join them in the bread, cheese and ale that Mistress

Foster laid out for them. It was simple fare, but all home made and to Hetty, far more delicious than the elaborate meals at Birch Hill.

After they'd eaten, Will excused himself, saying he had to ride out to Maidenhead and would not be back until late, but that he hoped Hetty would stay as long as she could, and come as often as she was able.

When Will had gone, Sophia said, 'Let me take you round the farm. And I have something to show you which I think you will like to see.'

Intrigued, Hetty let herself be taken out to the yard to see two working horses and a mule, stabled in one of the outhouses.

'Will has taken our best horse to ride out, but I know of an even better one. A beautiful black beast that no-one seems to know about,' Sophia said conspiratorially.

'You told me of a horse before,' Hetty said. 'A secret horse you called him. What did you mean? Is it a wild one?'

Sophia laughed. 'He's not a wild one, but he doesn't seem to have an owner. Well, I suppose he must have, but I don't know who that is.' She led Hetty round the back of the house, through a gate and across a field where cows were grazing.

At the far side of the field was a small coppice with a path leading through it. Sophia ran ahead, calling for Hetty to follow and plunged between the trees. Hetty had to lift her skirts to prevent them catching on brambles and encroaching bushes as she hurried to keep Sophia in sight. The coppice was larger than it had first appeared, and Hetty was sure she would have been hopelessly lost had she been by herself.

'Here we are!' Sophia stopped at last and Hetty saw they had reached a small clearing with a hut in the middle. Piled outside against the side of the hut were bales of straw and a leather bucket.

Sophia ran across the clearing towards the hut, calling eagerly to Hetty to come. She pulled open the door and disappeared inside. Hetty followed her, rather more hesitantly.

Inside it was dim, the only light coming from an open skylight high up in the roof. At first Hetty could see nothing, though there was a pungent smell of horse. Then she heard a rustle and a large, black shape loomed up near her.

She stepped back, startled, but Sophia had gone forward to fling her arms round a big black horse, hugging him and whispering endearments to him.

'Isn't he a beauty?' she said. 'He's the best horse I've ever seen! I wager he's as speedy as any, though I've never seen him run.'

'What's he doing here, in the middle of a wood? Surely someone must come and look after him?' Hetty asked. She reached up and stroked the great horse, who accepted her touch without flinching. Clearly, he was used to humans.

'He lives here. And I suppose someone owns him, since he is well cared for,' Sophia said, 'but I don't know who it can be. It can't be Will, or the horse would be in our stables with the others, but this is on the edge of our land, so anyone might have put up the hut years ago and used it as a stable. I've asked Will about it but he pretended he didn't know anything about this beauty, and told me there was only an old, empty hut here and I ought not to wander in the coppice as it was too far from home.'

'That's rather strange.' Hetty was getting used to the gloom now, and saw there was more straw in a pile in one corner, and a feeding trough and second water bucket. Someone must come here regularly, and exercise this horse, too, for he looked in excellent condition.

'Will told me I shouldn't come here as I might meet villagers in the woods, and he knew I wouldn't want to be seen,' Sophia continued. 'But I wanted to see the horse again, so I was always very careful and looked out for people, but I've never seen anyone here. And why should there be, when it borders our own land?'

She nuzzled the horse and he nodded his great head, used to her presence.

'I've never told anyone that I come here to see him. He's my friend, my only friend till you came to see me. He doesn't mind my face and I talk to him a lot. I don't know his name but I call him Star. D'you see?' She pointed up at the horse's head, where a white blaze in a diamond shape stood out on his forehead, the only part not completely black.

'Look, Star, I've brought my friend, Hetty, to see you,' she told the horse, turning his head towards Hetty. 'Would you like some more water, and see, I've brought you an apple.' She held out an apple on the flat of her hand and Star took it daintily, biting into it and demolishing it in a couple of mouthfuls.

Sophia picked up the water bucket and turned to the door, to refill it from the bucket outside. Hetty moved away from Star, who seemed a rather tall horse in such a confined space, so very much larger than Firefly. She sat down on the pile of straw in the corner and made to settle herself comfortably.

There was something hard underneath her, and she knelt up and brushed away a few handfuls. Her eyes widened in astonishment at what she had revealed. Hidden beneath the straw were a pair of flintlock pistols.

In spite of the gloom, there was no mistaking them. Hetty picked one up and turned it over in her hand. It looked a fearsome weapon and, apart from some dust from the straw, was clean and rust free. These weapons were not old and discarded, they had been kept ready for use.

She felt farther under the straw and unearthed a cloak, a tricorn hat and a long black scarf. There was no mistaking their use. No-one but a highwayman would have such things, kept hidden along with a speedy black horse.

She didn't know what to do, but instinct told her to cover the things again before Sophia came staggering back in with the heavy water bucket, now full.

Should she say anything? It seemed very much as if Sophia had not found any of these things, had no idea that this was the hideout of a highwayman. Being hidden away from everyone for most of her life, she probably had little idea about such people.

Hetty did not want to spoil her enjoyment of the lovely horse, or frighten her by telling her the truth. So long as she thought of the horse a secret and told no-one, Sophia would probably be safe, but such a ruthless robber would not take kindly to anyone discovering his hideout.

Perhaps she should persuade Sophia not to come here too often, yet in daylight she would surely be safe enough. Highwaymen rode out at night, under cover of darkness. They would not be abroad in the day.

'Sophia, had we not better go back to the farm and see your mother?' Hetty asked, scrambling to her feet. She glanced surreptitiously at the straw to make sure everything was well covered again. Sophia said goodbye to Star and obediently followed Hetty out of the hut.

'It's our secret now,' she said. 'I never told anyone, even Mama does not know about the hut in the woods. I am sure she would have spoken of it if she had.'

Hetty was quiet as they walked back, her mind in turmoil. It seemed inconceivable that Will could be one of the highwaymen who was responsible for holding up so many coaches recently, yet who else would keep such a horse and cloak and pistols, hidden on his land? If not Will himself, he must surely know more than he pretended?

'Hetty, you must come again very soon. In fact, I would like you to come and visit me every day,' Sophia demanded, when it was time to leave. 'I am still fearful to leave the farm and let people see me. I've looked in my mirror, as you bade me, and I confess it took much courage, but now I know what I really look like.

'You may say I am not so bad as I think, and maybe that it so, but I am scarred enough for folk to stare and I couldn't abide that. Come and visit and tell me all that is going on in the world, so that I may see it all through your eyes.'

★ ★ ★

When Hetty returned to Birch Hall, Margaret was in the drawing-room with Sir John. Sir George Astley had been visiting them and had just left.

'Hetty, where have you been?' Margaret asked. 'You never seem to be here when I want you, and it was discourteous to Sir George to be absent when he came.'

'I went to Foster's farm, to visit Will's sister, Sophia, and her mother. I am sorry if I was not here to greet Sir

George, but I thought he had come merely to talk business with Sir John,' Hetty replied.

'Foster's farm?' Margaret frowned. 'I did not know Will Foster had a sister. I have never heard of her. I am not sure if you should be visiting one of the local farmer's families. Will is hardly of our social standing . . . '

'Oh, Mama!' Hetty burst out, in concern. 'Sophia rarely leaves the farm and has no friends of her own. I heard of her from Will when I spoke to him at our party. It didn't occur to me that I should not visit the family of someone who had been a guest in our house.'

Margaret looked puzzled. 'Was Will Foster invited here?' She turned to Sir John. 'Surely, my dear, we only invited local people from the best families in the county? And Will Foster . . . '

'Will Foster is a good man,' Sir John said. He seemed in a jovial mood. 'Hetty will take no harm from visiting his mother, I am sure. I, too, admit that I never knew he had a sister. What like is she, Hetty? Why have we never heard of the girl?'

'Sophia is about my age, Sir. She is shy and, she has an affliction which makes her unwilling to leave the house,' Hetty explained.

'Then perhaps you do her a service by visiting,' Sir John replied.

Hetty gave him a grateful look. It would have been too much if she had been forbidden to visit Sophia, after Mama had shown disapproval of her continuing friendship with Mary Fletcher.

'Though I'm sure Sir George would have been pleased to see a pretty young face here to greet him, we had much serious business to attend to, and little time to be sociable,' Sir John continued. 'Not, of course, that we did not appreciate your presence to serve us refreshments, my dear,' he added to Margaret gallantly. 'Sir George and I have agreed on a plan to thwart these dastardly highway robbers and clear them from the county once and for all.'

'What are you going to do?' Hetty asked. She had a sinking feeling in the pit of her stomach.

'We intend to appeal to the loyalty and good sense of our law abiding citizens,' he said, rather pompously. 'Notices will be posted in every alehouse and village square, offering a bounty for information that will lead to the capture and conviction of any highway robber. Not that there won't be the one without the other, of course. They will certainly be convicted, once caught.'

'And then what will happen to them?'

'The gallows, of course. Strung up for all to see what happens to felons. The entertainment of a public execution should entice our local peasants to speak up if they had heard rumours, and the offer of five golden guineas for information leading to an arrest will tempt even the squeamish, I vow.'

'Do you think any villagers will come forward?' Hetty asked.

'For money, I doubt not. But there is

even more of an inducement; my own idea. There will be a pardon for any felon who turns King's Evidence and gives information leading to the apprehension of a highway robber.'

'You mean, if one of them betrays another, he will go free?' Hetty asked.

'Well, not quite. The proclamations we have had posted tell of a pardon for criminals, but that would only be for minor crimes. For others, the court may forgo the hanging but the alternative will be prison for life, and there are some who would say such a fate would be worse than death.'

Hetty had gone pale. Sir John noticed and patted her shoulder kindly.

'Nay, do not fret for such. The world and particularly this county will be well rid of them. Our main road through the thicket will be safe for travellers very soon now, I am sure.'

Hetty could not get the thought of Will out of her mind, and now, another worrying idea came to torment her. Ned had spoken of one day owning his own farm, even of being someone better than a farmer.

How would he ever be able to do that, unless he acquired more money than he could ever earn as a farm labourer? But if he was working with Will, not just on the farm, but as a highwayman — and the reports of the hold up had said there were two men involved — that would be the only way he could hope to amass a fortune, unless he was caught. And now, Sir John was determined that all highway robbers would be caught, and hanged.

She couldn't bear it. Hetty had to go and see Ned and find out if it was true. She slipped out of the house that evening before dinner and made her way on foot to the village and Mary Fletcher's cottage.

She did not want to risk riding Firefly as she would have had to explain where she was going.

Mary Fletcher greeted her like a long lost daughter and bade her sit by the fire and tell her all her news.

Hetty told her about visiting Will's sister and how they were now firm friends.

'The poor young girl,' Mary said. 'I mind when she caught the pox. A bonny child she was till then, and it struck her down just at the age when girls are self conscious of their appearance.

'I never had sight nor sound of her from that day till now. Some folks in their village thought she had died of it, and some said it would be better if she did, so terrible were the consequences. I'm so glad the little lass is beginning to accept that life must continue.'

'Where is Ned?' Hetty asked, looking round. She had hoped for a chance to speak to him, preferably alone.

'Ned works for Will Foster now. He stays there most nights, sleeping in their barn above the stables,' Mary said. 'I don't see him much these days, though he brings me money regularly. Will must pay him well, for Ned is always generous.'

Hetty's heart sank. It was beginning to sound as if her suspicions were right.

'Do you know what work Ned does?' she asked.

Mary looked surprised.

'Why, he helps on the farm, of course! What else would he do? Anything to do with looking after the animals, or growing crops. He's very busy, no time for childish games these days. He wouldn't have time for climbing trees and stealing rides on haycarts any more.'

She gave Hetty a sly smile.

'Aye, he told me about that incident. I couldn't believe a young lady like yourself would climb a tree or risk life and limb dropping off a branch on to a haycart passing beneath. I'll warrant your mama didn't hear the tale.'

'No, and I'd rather she never did,' Hetty replied quickly.

Margaret was becoming very conscious of her social standing these days, she would be horrified to hear about the haycart incident.

Surprisingly, Hetty felt sure that Sir John would have been amused rather than angry about it.

'I'm sorry to have missed Ned,' she said, preparing to leave. 'I was hoping he had found satisfactory work at last.'

'Oh, aye. He's pleased to be working with Will Foster. The man treats him well, in some ways more like a son than a mere labourer. From what Ned says, and the way Will is so generous to him, I wonder if in time to come he doesn't make our Ned a partner, being as how there are no other menfolk in Will's family, and Sophie unlikely to take a husband, with her affliction.'

A partner in what, Hetty thought uneasily. It was plain Mary Fletcher had no idea that Ned might be working in other ways than farm labouring, and there was no way that Hetty could see that she could warn Mary without frightening her on Ned's behalf.

'I'll have to go,' she said, standing up. 'Tell Ned when you see him that I wish him well, and — good luck, and to take good care of himself.'

'Aye, I'll do that. But likely you'll see him afore I do, if you visit Sophia at Foster's farm.' Mary laughed.

* * *

The next day, coming downstairs to the kitchens, Hetty was startled to see Abel Benson sitting in the chair in the passageway. He was in his boots and working clothes and there was a smug look on his face.

'Benson! What are you doing here?' Surely, he hadn't come to report her for the haycart incident, after all this time?

Benson leered at her as she stopped beside him.

'Happen I have business with Sir John,' he said importantly. 'Something I want to report to him. Something he'll be very pleased to hear about, I don't doubt.'

Hetty straightened up, putting on a haughty expression.

'If you've come to tell Sir John about

the haycart,' she began, 'then you needn't trouble yourself. He won't be interested. He'll be more interested in poachers, I'm sure.'

'Oh, I'm not telling about the 'aycart,' Benson said, with a nasty laugh. 'I've something much more important to say. And you needn't think he'll be interested in any poaching that might 'ave gone on around here, because that'll be pardoned on account of what I'm about to tell him.'

'And what is that?' A cold, sinking feeling was enveloping Hetty.

She saw that Abel Benson was clutching a sheet of paper in his hands, something she recognised only too well. She'd seen several just like it, posted up in the village on her way home from visiting Mary Fletcher.

AWARD OFFERED FOR INFOR-MATION LEADING TO THE CAPTURE OF ANYONE INVOLVED IN HIGH-WAY ROBBERY.

'Ar, that'd be telling.' Abel gave a sly grin. 'Reckon I'll be five guineas richer after I've spoken to Sir John, and he'll be inviting me to snare rabbits on his land, he'll be that grateful.'

Croker came along the passage from the direction of the main hall, and Sir John's study. He looked at Benson with some distaste.

'Sir John will see you now, Abel,' he said coldly. 'And see you wipe those boots of yours before you walk all over his lordship's fine rugs.'

Benson stood up. He smirked at Hetty, but there was something more in the look he gave her, a knowing look which seemed as if he had read her very thoughts.

6

Hetty watched Abel Benson follow Croker along the hall towards Sir John's door. How she longed to follow them and listen to what was being said! But that would have been impossible. The doors were thick and sound proof and, besides, Croker was hovering outside, waiting to escort Benson back to the kitchen quarters and out of the house, not trusting what the man might take a fancy to, if left alone.

She must go to the farm and warn Will, Hetty decided. She ran upstairs to change into her riding clothes, but hardly had she reached the first landing, when Margaret's maid Hawkins, called to her from Margaret's sitting room.

'Miss Hetty! Your mama says she wishes you to ride out with her in the carriage this morning. She is making a visit and you are to accompany her.'

'Oh, but I — ' It was not wise to argue with Mama, but still Hetty went into the pretty sitting room that was Margaret's own domain, to plead with her.

'I promised I would visit Sophia as often as I could,' she said. 'The poor girl is very lonely, and she depends on me for company.'

'Heavens, Hetty! Sophia can surely exist one day without you! She had years and years of managing herself before she even knew of your existence!' Margaret said briskly. 'I am going to visit my cousin in Maidenhead and of course you must come as well. Cousin Emma will certainly want to see you.

'It was at her house that I met Sir John again after all those years since your father died, and had it not been for Emma — well, let us say that I shall always be eternally grateful to her for her hospitality on that occasion. Come, be quick and put on your best clothes, child. She must see that her help to us has borne fruit and that we are now very well cared for.'

Really, Mama was becoming far too concerned with appearances and social standing, Hetty thought morosely. She had never been like this, even when Papa had been alive and they had been, if not as rich as Sir John, at least not as poor as they rapidly became after his death.

And Maidenhead! It would take most of the morning to reach there. She could not possibly hope to see Will before the late afternoon now.

Hetty was tempered to feign a headache, or some such ailment to avoid the trip, but then it would be difficult to ride out to Foster's farm without anyone knowing. Hawkins would undoubtedly see and report her.

With a bad grace, Hetty gave in and went to put on something suitable for the visit. When she and Margaret came downstairs to leave, Sir John came out of his study, looking very pleased with himself.

'Well, my dear, I've had a good morning's work today,' he announced, rubbing his hands together with satisfaction. 'I've had a response from all those notices I had posted about the village. Abel Benson has been to see me, with some very useful information.'

'Abel Benson? That unpleasant creature! What could he have to tell you?' Margaret asked. 'I wouldn't believe a word that man said.'

'Maybe not, my dear. But you dislike him because he mixes with some of the low life of the country, which is exactly why anything he says could be of value. He knows a good deal of what goes on around here, and he's not above reporting things — if he's tempted by sufficient reward.

'I flatter myself my little ruse has worked and Abel Benson had been persuaded to give me enough information to catch at least one, if not two, of our robbers, all for the sake of a paltry five guineas, plus the promise that the courts will turn a blind eye to a minor misdemeanour regarding a few rabbits on Sir George's land.'

'You mean — you are actually going to catch these dreadful highway robbers?' Margaret asked. She looked quite pale with shock, masking the fact that Hetty, too, had turned white.

'Not myself personally, of course.' Sir John gave a deprecating little chuckle. 'I'm off this very moment to put wheels in motion, so to speak. Alert the men of the Watch and my own men, too, so that they will all be ready. I can guarantee that tonight's Bath coach will be the very last these villains will attempt to hold up, and that by tomorrow's dawn they will be in the lock up, awaiting the next Assizes — and then the gallows.'

'Tonight — highwaymen are going to attempt to hold up tonight's mail coach?' Hetty whispered.

'Aye, but they aren't going to succeed. My men will be waiting for them!' Sir John looked very pleased with himself.

'Where are they going to waylay them?' She couldn't help herself asking.

Sir John gave a patronising chuckle.

'Ah! That would be telling wouldn't it? There needs to be absolute secrecy about this operation. I couldn't tell even you, my dears. But you'll know all about it by tomorrow morning, for sure. Now, be off with you both and have a safe journey to Maidenhead. And give my humble respects to cousin Emma, won't you, Margaret, and tell her, next time she's a fancy to take a coach along the Bath Road in this direction, she can feel as safe as if she was taking a turn round her own village green.'

Gallantly, he handed Margaret into the waiting carriage and helped Hetty in beside her. Then he was off, striding towards the stables and already calling for Thomas to saddle his horse.

She simply had to warn Will before tonight! And Ned, too, for now, because of what Mary Fletcher had said, Hetty was convinced that Ned was just as much involved.

The only thing she could think of was to plead that she felt unwell, and try to persuade Mama to cut short her visit and return earlier than planned. If she had to escape from the house after they returned, then so be it.

Whatever happened afterwards, Hetty had to stop Will from holding up the coach tonight and falling into the trap that was being set for him.

★ ★ ★

Hetty endured the agony of sitting through the tedium of making small talk to cousin Emma for most of the late morning. She tried complaining of feeling unwell, but cousin Emma merely suggested lying down with a cloth soaked in lavender water across her forehead.

There was no way of escaping then, for it would have been too far to try to travel back to Burchetts Green without transport, so she had to wait while Mama made her protracted farewells to cousin Emma, telling her that the roads would be safe at last, there was no excuse for her not to come for a visit to Birch Hall. Hetty knew that her mother had wanted to show off her new home to her Maidenhead relative, and now was the perfect opportunity.

At last, they were back in the carriage again and on their way home. The autumn sun was low on the horizon and Hetty knew she would have to hurry if she was not to arrive at Foster's farm before dark. What would they think of her, visiting so late? She couldn't explain why, for Sophia and her mother must never know what work Will did after dark, when his farm work was over.

Margaret was fatigued by the carriage ride, and decided to rest in her room until dinner, so she barely noticed when Hetty ran upstairs and into her own room.

In seconds she had changed from her best clothes into something suitable for riding, and had slipped down the back stairs and out of the side door, running for the stables.

Thomas was eating his evening meal in the stable, but jumped up at once to saddle Firefly as soon as Hetty burst in on him.

'Why, what's the matter, Miss Hetty?' he asked. ''Tis getting near dusk for a ride out now.'

'I don't care! Just saddle him! And I'm going alone!' Hetty demanded. She looked so determined and fierce that Thomas didn't argue. Miss Hetty was a headstrong young lady at the best of times, so he let her have her way. He just hoped Sir John didn't blame him for anything afterwards.

Hetty rode as fast as she dared in the gathering dusk. When she neared Foster's farm, she slowed and dismounted near the gate, where she tethered Firefly. Trying to appear as casual as possible, she came round to the back of the farm and knocked on the back door, as she usually did. Sophia came running to open it for her.

'Hetty! You've come so late! I had given up expecting you long since!' she said.

'I had to go to Maidenhead in the carriage with Mama, to visit her cousin, but I wanted to come afterwards, only it took forever for them to take leave of each other.' Hetty explained. 'Where is Will? I have a message for him.'

'Our Will is away to Newbury today,' said Mistress Foster, coming into the kitchen. 'He walked to the crossroads to pick up the noon coach, and he will be staying there overnight, he said. He has some business to attend to.'

'He's not here? He's already gone?' Hetty said, stunned.

'Be back tomorrow, very early, he said. The message can surely wait until then,' Mistress Foster said easily.

'Sophia,' Hetty said, as soon as her mother had gone to fetch ale and cheese for them all, 'will you take me

130

out to the coppice to see Star? I have a fancy to look at the horse again.'

'But it's nearly dark,' Sophia objected.

'We could take a lantern.'

'I don't need a lantern. I know these woods well. I was thinking of you. I'm used to walking at night. There is no-one likely to see me then,' Sophia said. 'Come on, if you really want to, we can go quickly before Mama has laid out our supper.'

★   ★   ★

Hetty was breathless as they ran across the fields towards the little wood, breathless with anxiety as well as the speed they were making. Sophia plunged into the wood and Hetty followed her.

Perhaps they would be in time and Will would not have collected his horse, if indeed Star was his horse. She would leave a message tied to his bridle.

Sophia ran ahead and flung open the door of the hut. Then she stopped, and Hetty nearly cannoned into her.

'Star isn't here,' she said in astonishment. 'But he's always been here when I've come before.'

Hetty stepped into the hut and went as casually as she could over to the pile of straw. She stepped over it, scuffing her feet through it. She could not feel any lumps or bumps underneath the straw. The cloak, tricorn hat and pistols had all been taken, along with Star.

'That's very strange. Whoever owns him must have taken him near dusk,' Sophia said. 'I was in the wood earlier but I didn't see anyone.'

'Have you seen Ned today? Is he working somewhere on the farm?' Hetty asked.

'Ned? No, not since early when he came to do the milking. I think Will must have said he could take some time off to visit his mother, since he himself would not be here.'

It was clear that Sophia had no idea why Will had said he was travelling to Newbury.

'Oh, he has business in that town

sometimes,' she said, shrugging. 'Maybe he wants to look at some beasts to buy, or find out the best prices for selling. He often goes away overnight, but he is always back early next day.'

* * *

Hetty ate some cheese and bread that Mistress Foster pressed upon her, but she was distracted by thinking what she could do now. As soon as she could, she took her leave, pleading that it was now almost completely dark and she must hurry home.

'You'll never ride back in the dark?' Mistress Foster said anxiously. 'Stay with us tonight. If Will were here he would ride you back, but there's no menfolk here at present.'

'I must get home. Mama will expect me. I shall be safe enough, I know the roads well by now and soon the moon will have risen. That will give me plenty of light.' She was fidgeting now to go, as a plan was beginning to form in her mind.

'Aye, the moon will be up before you are back. A full moon tonight. The main road to Bath will be as bright as day, though your lanes may still be dark with the overshadowing trees,' Mistress Foster said.

In spite of knowing the lanes well, Hetty rode slowly and carefully back towards Birch Hall. If Firefly were to trip and pull a muscle again, as he had done the day they'd met the gypsy girl, Hetty knew she would have a big problem in carrying out her plan, let alone arriving home before she was missed by Mama.

She had to cross the Bath road to take the lane leading to Birch Hall, and by then the moon was giving sufficient light to see along the empty road in both directions. The trees had been cut back beside the road, leaving a grassy verge some six feet or so wide, but beyond that the bushes and under-growth were thick and dense, excellent cover for men hiding in wait for a coach, and a full moon would give them all the light they needed to see the coach and its occupants clearly.

With a full moon there was less chance that one of the guards could load and fire a pistol without being seen, or escape to raise the alarm.

Croker had explained to her how it was that moonlit nights were the most dangerous for the coaches that came from London making the night run to arrive in Newbury or Reading in time for an early breakfast.

If only I knew where they planned to stop the coach, she thought. There were at least two miles of road running through the thicket, and almost any part of it was open to ambush. The only thing she could do would be to ride along the length of the road on the grass verge so that Firefly's hoofbeats didn't sound, and hope that she would find Will and Ned hidden away just inside the covering bushes.

She turned Firefly away from the lane to Birch Hall and on to the side of the main road. He was reluctant to go, knowing the lane led to home and a warm stable, but she encouraged him with whispered words and persuaded him to trot softly and slowly on the grass, while she peered into the darkness on each side of her.

This was hopeless. Will and Ned could be lying in wait a dozen yards from her and she would never see them. Of course, they would be making sure that any lone horseman wouldn't see them, and raise the alarm. She didn't dare call out to them and she was beginning to feel alone and rather frightened.

They might have missed her at home by now and would be demanding answers when she returned. She couldn't give any satisfactory explanation of why she was out so late, but she couldn't turn back now, whatever it meant. She wasn't going to abandon Will and Ned to certain capture and death on the gallows.

The road was dipping slightly and

she knew that a short way farther on it bent to the left in a slight curve to cross over the bridge of a small stream, then began to rise on a steady incline before levelling out again. Of course! That would be the place anyone wanting to halt a coach would choose!

The horses would have to slow down to take the bend and prepare for the incline, and the coachman would be momentarily distracted by the bridge. That would be the moment to spring out and stop them. Now she realised it, that had been the very spot where the carriage of the hapless Lady Mountjoy had been waylaid.

Hetty urged Firefly forward. The coach would probably come through within the next hour and she had to find Will and Ned and warn them to leave, ride as far away from the road as possible. It was likely Sir John might have ordered constables of the Watch to be lying in wait for them, too, and she must persuade them to go before they were seen by anyone.

The road began its wide curve towards the left and the low parapet of the bridge could just be seen. Which side of the road would they likely to hide? It would be beyond the bridge, she thought, but here was a problem. There was no grass verge over the bridge and if she rode Firefly across he would certainly be heard, if not seen as well.

The waiting highwaymen would move back into the denseness of the thicket to avoid being seen and she would never find them. The only way was to dismount and creep through the bushes on foot, coming upon them from the other direction.

Hetty dismounted and drew Firefly to the edge of the trees, tying him to a branch in a place where he could find grass to munch. He tossed his head, clearly puzzled by her behaviour. She patted him and whispered, 'Be quiet, now. I'll be back for you soon. I'm not leaving you for long.'

They'd come upon the coach from

the inner side of the bend, she decided, which meant she had to cross the road, bathed in bright moonlight now. The best way would be to cross the bridge, hoping the parapet would provide some shadow. They couldn't be far away now.

Hetty was still on the wrong side of the road, walking carefully close beside the bushes when she thought she heard a cough. She stopped, listening and trying to identify the direction of the sound. It came from this side of the road, and for a moment she was puzzled, then worried.

Could they be Sir John's constables of the Watch in place already, waiting for Will and Ned to hold up the coach? She didn't dare try to cross the road at this point, for anyone hiding nearby would see her clearly, and now she feared it wouldn't be Will.

Quietly, Hetty edged forward. As her eyes became used to the gloom of the undergrowth, she thought she saw something move, and then, unmistakably, came the snort of a horse. It was very close, closer than she had expected. Hetty moved a little farther forward and found a gap in the bushes, large enough for a horse to push through.

She turned into it, and saw that behind the bushes edging the verge was a small clearing running back, parallel with the road, and in it, not more than a dozen feet away, she could make out the outlines of two horses, with a cloaked figure on the back of each.

'Will! Will Foster!' Hetty whispered, as loud as she dared. She saw the figure on the taller horse jerk upright and swivel round. The silhouette of an arm holding a pistol rose up against the greyness of the night.

'Who's that?' the voice was sharp, but it was unmistakably that of Will himself.

'It's Hetty. Hetty Neville. Don't shoot me, please. Is that Ned with you?'

'Hetty! What in God's name are you doing here?' Will spoke angrily.

'I know you're planning to hold up the Bath coach. I've come to warn you. Sir John knows about it and has set a trap for you. There'll be constables waiting to arrest you if you try to do anything. Quickly, ride away now, as far as you can. Sir John doesn't know who the robbers are but if you stay here they'll find you and you'll be caught. He's sworn to hang you if he does.' Hetty's voice caught a sob. 'Will, save yourself, please! And Ned, too! I couldn't bear it if — ' she stopped, unable to finish.

'Ned, take Hetty back to Birch Hall on the back of your horse. He'll carry you both. If you're quick you can be back before this coach is due.' Will ordered sharply. 'I don't doubt she'll know how to slip indoors without anyone knowing of this escapade.'

'No!' Hetty grabbed hold of Will's horse's bridle and pulled at it. She was hardly surprised to see that it was Star, the horse from the hut in the woods.

'Hetty, do as you're told.'

'I'm not going to let you be caught and hanged! I'll stop you myself, somehow!' There was no way she could hold back the big black horse, but she would have to try, if Will didn't see sense and give up this madness.

There was a strange sound coming from Will's throat, a sound she couldn't understand, until she realised — it was the sound of laughter, the rich, hearty sound of a man who had just been told the most amusing story he had heard in a long time.

'Oh, Hetty! My lovely, brave Hetty! You came out here, all by yourself, to try to save me from the law men and constables? Only a girl like you, brave enough to drop from a high branch on to a moving haycart, brave enough to stand up to a man like Abel Benson, would do something like this!'

Hetty was so angry she hit out at Will, but he was so far above her on the tall horse that she could reach no farther than his leg, and made the horse lurch forward and skitter.

'Will! This is no laughing matter! Go, please, before it's too late! Ned, make him go! At least, go yourself. What will become of Mary, if you are arrested and hanged for highway robbery?' She was crying with exasperation, and fear for them both. There wasn't much time and —

'Hetty, do you really think we are a pair of highway robbers lying in wait to hold up the Bath coach?' Will's voice still burbled with laughter. 'I should be angry at such an accusation. Ned and I are here because we are Sir John's agents, waiting to catch the men who plan a real robbery.'

'What?' Hetty stared uncomprehendingly.

'Sir John had information laid that the Bath coach was to be attacked this night. He had his agents, secret men who lay in wait to trap the robbers. Ned and I have worked together on the roads for some time now, watching the highway, protecting coaches. We have not had such definitive information as this before, and we were sure of success this time, but now you are causing us a problem. It is too dangerous for you to be here. You must let Ned take you back to Birch Hall and safety, before trouble starts.'

'You — you are not — ' Hetty was still staring. 'But you hid your horse in a secret place in the woods, where you had pistols, and a cloak and mask, just like a highwayman would have.'

'Not such a secret place, if you found it, it would seem,' Will said ruefully. 'I think it may have been young Sophia who discovered it, and shared the secret with you. But have you not thought, not only highwaymen dress like this? We, too, need black cloaks and hats so that we can remain hidden in the shadows, and we are both masked because if it were known who we were, do you imagine that the robbers would let us still live? The life of a known agent of the law is short indeed. I could not even risk letting my mother or sister know the truth. Can I trust you?'

'Of course you can! I would do anything to protect you! Haven't I shown that already?' Hetty spoke more passionately than she realised.

Will reached down to her, clasping her hand.

'Well, then, let Ned take you home. Get up behind him, but be quick about it, for the coach is nearly due.'

'Firefly is tethered a little way back, by the verge. I shall have to ride him back,' Hetty explained.

As she spoke, they were alerted by the sounds of pistol shots along the road behind them, and a commotion of shouts, whinnying horses and crashing of wheels.

'God's teeth!' Will exclaimed. 'They have attacked the coach a mile farther back! The information was false! Quick, Ned, we must ride out and stop them before it's too late!'

7

Will and Ned wheeled their horses round and thrust through the gap in the bushes. Turning back towards the direction from which the coach was expected, they galloped away down the road towards the commotion. Will turned in his saddle to call to her.

'Hetty! Ride back to your home now! There is too much danger here for you!' Then they were gone, along the road and out of sight.

Hetty ran after them, calling to Firefly, and found him just a few yards along, in no way disturbed by the shouting and shots in the distance. She scrambled up into the saddle, using a fallen log to help her, and set her horse to follow the others along the road. She gave no thought to any possible danger to herself and it never occurred to her that she should have obeyed Will's instructions and ridden back to Birch Hall.

There was going to be excitement such as was rarely seen by ordinary citizens, certainly not by young women who ought to be asleep in their beds at such an hour. She wasn't going to miss anything, even if it meant Mama and Sir John never forgave her.

She saw the coach straddled across the road some way ahead. She slowed Firefly and led him on to the grass verge out of sight. When she was fifty yards or so away, she stopped and drew into the shadow of the undergrowth to see what was happening.

There was a man on horseback brandishing a pair of pistols, one in each hand and both pointed at the coach. The coachman had been forced to descend from his seat and a second man, who had dismounted from his horse, was tying him to the shafts of the coach.

Two other men who had been riding outside at the back of the coach had already had their hands tied behind their backs. One, who must have been wounded trying to resist, was lying groaning on the ground. A little group of passengers stood against the side of the coach, cowering in fear. They consisted of two ladies, one middle-aged and the other some ten years younger; a young girl who might have been maid to one of them, an elderly gentleman and a small child.

None of them appeared to be in any way capable of defending themselves, or defying the highwaymen. They were huddled together, rigid with fear, watching the robbers with wide, terrified eyes. Hetty watched as Will and Ned rode up, pistols drawn, demanding that the man on horseback drop his weapons.

He swivelled round in his saddle to face them, pointing his pistol at Will. Hetty gasped in horror, then threw her hands up to her face as there came a loud report and a flash of fire. When she dared look again, the man on horseback had dropped his pistol, was clutching his arm and shouting in pain. Will must have been a superb shot for he had fired directly at the pistol itself, putting a bullet through the man's hand.

'Ned — call out the Watch!' Will shouted, and almost at once Hetty heard a series of shrill blasts on a whistle, followed by an echoing reply from deep within the thicket and, moments later, several men rode out along the road from the opposite direction.

By the time they had pulled up beside the coach, Will had forced the rider to dismount and was tying his hands behind his back, while Ned was securing the second man.

'Here, they're all yours now, men!' Will called triumphantly. Ropes were produced and the two highwaymen lashed to the saddles of two of the Watch's horses. Another man took charge of the two spare horses, leading them either side of his own.

'Take them directly to the lock-up, lads,' Will ordered. 'They can go before the Magistrate in the morning.' He turned his attention to the coachman, unfastening him from the shafts. 'Are you hurt, Coachman?' he asked. 'Shaken up, I don't doubt. I suggest you return to the local inn and rest there until daybreak.'

'No, no. I have the mail and other goods to take onwards. We cannot be late,' the coachman insisted. He looked at his two colleagues, whom Ned had released. 'What do you think, lads? Now our heroes have captured these highwaymen, we shall surely be safe to continue to Newbury.'

'Samuel here is injured,' said one, indicating the man on the ground. 'We should get him to a doctor as soon as possible.' He looked at the passengers, still cowering against the side of the coach. 'You'll not easily get them to continue far, after this encounter,' he muttered.

Hetty had dismounted from Firefly

and moved quietly forward. On the grass and against the undergrowth she had not been noticed but now she came up to the two ladies of the party and clasped their hands comfortingly.

'Ladies, are you all right? You have not been hurt?' she asked. She bent down to the child and lifted her into her arms. 'There, there, little one. There is nothing to be afraid of now. The nasty men have been taken away and you are quite safe.'

'Lord save us! Is the Watch employing females now!' the elderly gentleman exclaimed. 'We shall have to be very brave so as not to lose face in front of such Amazons.'

'And you, Sir? Are you unharmed? Shocked and upset I'm sure, as you all must be. There is an inn barely half a mile distant and you would be well received there. If you do not want to continue travelling tonight, whether or not the coachman continues, you could always take rooms for the night and travel on in the morning coach, making the rest of your journey by daylight. I think you will have to make a stop at the inn in any case, to let this poor fellow who has been injured, be attended to.'

'It's nobbut a scratch, Miss,' Samuel said, sitting up on the side of the road. His companion was helping him off with his coat and rolling up his sleeve for him. 'The ball grazed my arm and it's nothing that a piece of bandage won't set right. I was writhing and moaning a lot in the hope of distracting the villains. I thought as how they might take fright and ride off, if they thought they'd injured me badly.'

'A brave fellow,' Will commented. 'Am I to understand that we arrived in time, and you have not been parted from your valuables? I saw nothing in the men's hands but their guns, and the Watch will have searched them before they dragged them away.'

'They made us alight from the coach, but they were more interested in the chests and boxes on the coach roof,' said the old gentleman. 'Once they saw who we were, they rightly guessed there would be little of value to be had from us. I am Mr John Webster,' he made a little bow towards Will. 'And this is my wife, Amelia, and her younger sister, Jane. We were travelling to Marlborough with Jane's little daughter, Charlotte, and our maid, Betsy. Sir, I dread to think what might have happened had you not arrived in such a timely fashion. Those villains might have murdered us all, if they had taken a notion to do so.'

'We were glad to be of service. I am Will Foster, a local farmer hereabouts, as well as Sir John Lattimore's special agent, charged with guarding our notorious thicket. And this is my assistant, Ned Fletcher.'

'And is the young woman your assistant, too? I admire her bravery in coming with you in such a dangerous situation,' Mr Webster said.

'Hetty!' Will rounded on her. He had not noticed her presence before. 'I thought I told you to ride home at once! This is no place for a young woman!'

'I thought I might be of particular help to any ladies who might have been distressed by the hold up,' Hetty said guilelessly.

Will merely stared at her in amazement.

'I suppose I shall have to escort you back to Birch Hall myself and try to explain to Sir John and your mother what you were doing, involving yourself with highwaymen at dead of night,' he said. 'I doubt not that Sir John will be very angry, and your mother outraged.'

'I think they would be even angrier if they knew the real reason I came looking for you,' Hetty murmured, but so quietly that Will was not sure he heard correctly. He would hardly have known how to answer if he had, so contented himself by scowling at her. Really, how on earth was one supposed to cope with a wench as independent and wayward as she!

The coachman agreed to drive on to

the local inn and leave his passengers there overnight, deciding his own plans when a doctor had examined his colleague. The horses had suffered a shock, too, being startled and forced to stop suddenly, and a change would be prudent, whether or not he continued that night.

The two other members of the Watch rode beside the coach as escort and to show them the way. Will and Ned watched them drive on slowly through the last mile of the thicket to the turn off for the inn.

'Hetty, where have you left your pony?'

Hetty pointed behind them, towards the undergrowth.

'He's safe. I left him having an extra meal of grass.'

'It seems he might have been the only one who was safe tonight, then,' Will muttered crossly. 'Fetch him, Hetty, and let's be on our way to face the wrath of Sir John and your mother.'

Hetty ran along the side of the road

but she had barely gone half a dozen paces when she fell over something lying hidden in the grass, sprawling her length on the ground and scraping her shins on a sharp, metallic edge.

'What now?' Will came forward to help her to her feet. 'Not a swoon, Hetty, after all that excitement?'

'No, of course not! I fell over something.' Hetty rubbed at her legs. 'It wasn't a log, it felt sharp, more like metal.'

'Ned, bring your tinderbox and candle!' Will called. He knelt down where Hetty had fallen and ran his hands over the object. ' 'Tis a box, a metal box! Perhaps this came from the coach and they did not realise their loss. Quick, Ned, let us have light to see what is here!'

Ned was already lighting a stump of candle from the smouldering shreds of cloth in the tinderbox, and brought it close to where the other two crouched in the grass.

'It's unlocked! Open it, Will,' Ned

urged. Will undid the catch and threw the lid back. Ned held the candle high over it, and gasped.

'Jewels! And money! There's a fortune here!' He exclaimed. 'Look, Hetty, here's a necklace fifty times more beautiful than that pendant Will told me of, so ugly yet worth a king's ransom! I'll wager you could ransom a whole city, a whole country with riches like these!'

Ned was taking the jewels from the box as he spoke, throwing necklaces and pendants round Hetty's neck until the weight of them pressed down on her chest.

'If you had these beauties, you could buy yourself an estate ten times bigger than Birch Hall. And look at this!' He plunged both hands deep into the box and scooped up a double handful of gold coins. 'With just this much I could buy myself a farm and have all the labourers working on it that I needed.

'I could be a gentleman of leisure and spend my days in dining and riding to hounds, and make my mother a lady wearing silks and satins and taking tea with the nobility of the county.'

'Oh, Ned!' Hetty knew what his dream had been and felt for him. She looked down at the rows of jewels, some still round her neck and some piled into her hands and she remembered the words of Meg, the gypsy girl who had read her palm. 'You will hold riches of great value in your hands but they are not to keep. You will never own them — you must never keep them or you will rue the day.'

What else had she said? Danger, and trouble. Well, there had certainly been danger this night, for all of them and there would be trouble soon, when she arrived back at Birch Hall. It would soon be dawn and she could never hope to creep back into the house undetected once the household was awake.

'Ned, don't even think such thoughts!' Will spoke sternly. 'You are paid well enough as my assistant so let that suffice. This chest must have been the first thing the robbers took before we disturbed them, and nobody noticed. We shall have to take it to the inn and hope the coachman has not decided to drive on already.'

'That you will not do!' An angry voice from the interior of the thicket startled them. Will turned round sharply and Hetty and Ned looked up. There was a dark shape standing no more than a dozen feet from them, cloaked in black, a tricorn hat on his head and a scarf masking the lower half of his face. In his hand he held a pistol and it was pointing directly at them.

'Another highwayman!' Will exclaimed. 'Surely you have not escaped from the Watch?'

The masked man gave a scornful laugh.

'Of course not! I have been watching it all from within the bushes. Why should I have appeared and been taken by your amateur law enforcers? My partners are taken but I still have my freedom and enough riches to start a new life, far from here. Now, be good enough to close that chest — with all its contents inside — and move away, or I shall have no hesitation in shooting Will Foster here, who has been a thorn in my flesh these months past.

'It will be a pleasure, I do assure you, Will, to put a bullet through your heart before I depart on your horse, which I know to be the speediest in the county. In fact, since I will be long gone before you can raise any alarm, I might as well shoot you anyway, in return for the lives of my partners, for you have ensured that they will be hanged for tonight's events. But I will not be hanged!' He raised his pistol, pointing it directly at Will's heart.

Hetty gasped. He meant what he said, that was clear. She couldn't let Will die. What would Sophia do without her brother to look after her and protect her from the world? Without Will the Fosters would lose their farm; be destitute like she and Margaret had been when her father died. And there would be no rich landowner like Sir John to help them. And, more than that, would what she do if Will was shot right here in front of her? She simply couldn't stay there and let it happen.

Slowly, Hetty got to her feet and lifted the necklaces from around her neck. She began to walk slowly towards the highwayman, holding them out towards him.

'Here you are, then. Take them,' she said.

'Hetty — what are you doing?' Will said anxiously. The highwayman hesitated, and she could see his eyes above the scarf were puzzled.

'I want it all, all that's in the chest,' he said. Hetty was now no more than two paces from him, standing directly between him and Will. He had lowered the pistol but it was still pointing in the same direction, aimed now at her. Suddenly she sprang forward, hurling the handful of jewellery at his face.

Startled, he stepped back and Hetty's

hand reached for the scarf. She tore at it and it came away in her hand. She just had time to see the man's entire face in the moonlight, just time to scream out his name.

'Abel Benson!' when there was a flash, a loud explosion and everything around her went black.

8

Hetty lay in a warm cocoon, gradually swimming into consciousness, wondering where she was, what had happened to her. Memory was gradually returning, and with it a host of questions she couldn't answer.

She had been sitting on the side of the main Bath road, the part leading through the notorious Maidenhead thicket, and the moon had been shining down. Ned and Will Foster had been there, too, and Ned had been draping jewels on her, hanging pendants and necklaces round her neck. But there had been a voice somewhere, a gypsy girl's voice, telling her, 'Not to keep. You will never own such baubles.'

Then there had been a great noise, then nothing. No, all that couldn't be right. She must have dreamed it all. She opened her eyes and saw she was in her own bed in her room at Birch Hall, so it must have been a dream. In the background she heard the sound of someone weeping.

'Mama?' Hetty tried to move and a searing pain shot through her arm, warning her it was better to lie still.

There was someone beside the bed now, her mother, but what was wrong? Mama was crying and looking at her with an expression Hetty had never seen on her face before.

'Hetty! You wicked girl! What did you think you were doing, going out at night by yourself and nearly getting yourself killed by a dreadful highwayman?'

Mama was sobbing uncontrollably and Hetty was relieved to see Sir John come to put an arm round her shoulders.

'Now, now, Margaret, my dear. Do not distress yourself. Hetty has regained consciousness at last and the doctor tells us her injuries will mend in time. We don't know the whole story from her yet, but it seems that, though she has behaved in a most unseemly manner, yet she has shown grave bravery. Heroism, in fact.'

'But she could have been killed!' Margaret wailed.

'Yes, indeed. It would appear that might have been so. But she has not been killed, as you can see for yourself, so take heart my dear. And remember what the doctor said — Hetty should not be troubled or questioned too much until she is more herself. Bring her some broth or a posset, to help her regain her strength quicker.'

Margaret moved away from Hetty's line of sight, and Sir John came nearer, to stand at the foot of the bed.

'Well, this is a rum do, and no mistake. Can you recall exactly what happened, Hetty? For I've heard such a tale from Will Foster and young Ned that I can scarcely credit.' He was looking down at her but he didn't seem as angry as Hetty had feared.

165

* * *

Things were beginning to come back to her. She had thought Will Foster was a highwayman, and had crept out at night to warn him, because Sir John and Sir George Astley had set a trap and she couldn't bear the thought of Will going up before the Assizes and being hanged.

And why had she risked so much to try to save him? It wasn't because Sophia would be devastated by such news, it was because she loved Will with all her heart and life without him would not be life at all.

She couldn't explain that to Sir John, and hoped he wasn't going to ask. He'd told her mother not to ask too many questions yet, but it looked as if he was about to do just that.

'What happened?' she asked. Things were still hazy in her mind. Of course, Will hadn't been a highwayman. He and Ned had been part of the trap set to catch them and she had somehow become bound up in it all.

'Will Foster brought you home at dawn two days ago, with a bullet lodged in your shoulder,' Sir John said. 'He and Ned Fletcher were lying in wait down by the bridge where the road bends, in the middle of the thicket, because I had been given information that the London to Bath coach was to be held up at that point that night.

'Then, out of nowhere, you appeared and called to them. I cannot think what you had in mind but I know you are an adventure-seeking girl, a child unlike what your mama would wish. You should have been born a boy.'

So Will had said nothing about her real reason for being there! Hetty sighed with relief.

'Your craving for excitement will lead you into untold trouble. Well, it has already, as you see. You will have to lie in your bed for several days yet, until your shoulder mends. And I doubt your mother will ever forgive you. She will always be minded that the bullet missed your heart by very little. And Will tells me that, had you not been there, the bullet would surely not have missed his heart.'

'I'm sorry, Sir John, for all the trouble I've caused you and Mama,' Hetty whispered humbly.

'Ah, well. You must make your peace with your mother as best you can. It may be in time that she will forgive, though I fear she will never forget, or let you do so.'

He smiled suddenly. 'Hetty, I said you should have been born a boy. I always wanted a son and if I had one, I would have been glad if he had been like you. Never let your mother hear that I said as much. She will not want me to encourage you, and certainly I would never want you to court danger in such a way again. But — I am proud of what you did that night.'

She had never before experienced the warm glow that spread throughout her whole being. Sir John had always seemed a cold, rather aloof man. Now, she knew that she'd share a closeness with him that even Mama wouldn't have.

'It was Abel Benson, wasn't it?' she said drowsily. She was remembering more and more, but the strain of talking was making her tired.

'It was indeed. The scoundrel tricked me into believing that he had information overheard at the inn, about our highwayman. Of course he had, he was the leader of the gang of them! But he gave me false information, set the scene for the hold up a mile away, making sure that my men, my agents for law and order and all the members of the Watch, were at the wrong place.

'Abel was even more cunning than that, though. While his men held up the coach and found no-one of wealth on board, he ordered them to take down a certain chest which he knew was bound for Bath with a fortune inside.

'As he instructed, they took it down first, while he waited under cover of the bushes in the thicket. He stayed where he was and actually watched his own men being arrested and marched off at the end of a rope tied to a horse's saddle.

'His plan was to escape abroad that very night but, thanks to you, his plan failed. His men told all when they realised Abel had tricked them out of all the valuable spoils from that coach. I heard word not an hour ago that he had been apprehended at Southampton trying to board a ship bound for the Americas.'

Margaret came back into the room with a maid carrying a tray.

'Can you eat a little soup, Hetty?' she asked. 'You must not tire yourself by fretting about these dreadful highway robbers. Leave all that to Sir John and Sir George.'

★ ★ ★

It was much later, Hetty was unsure whether it was the same day or not, so drowsy was she due to the pain-killing draught the doctor had left for her, that

Margaret came into the sunlight-filled room and told her that she had a visitor.

'Well, two visitors, actually. Young Ned has been here daily, asking after you, but of course I could not allow him to see you in your room. But Mary Fletcher has come and brought some-one with her.'

'Mistress Fletcher, dear Mary, I am so pleased to see you!' Hetty said. 'And is Ned well and safe? I don't remember what happened after Abel Benson fired his pistol.'

'Aye, Ned is well enough and glad to be playing the part of the hero who captured the highwaymen and made all safe in the thicket for travellers.' Mary laughed. 'He'll earn himself a few pennies telling that story for many months to come. Hetty, I have brought someone to see you, and when you see who it is you will know how important you have become in people's lives, that they want to go to such lengths to see for themselves you are safe now.'

Mary moved to the back of the room and drew forward a figure who was wrapped in a cloak with a scarf covering its entire face. As soon as she saw it, Hetty nearly screamed.

'It's Abel Benson! He had a mask like that!'

'Abel's in the lock-up in Southampton, waiting to be returned here to face the hangman,' Mary said. 'No, you are safe from him.'

'You've brought Ned then, disguised because Mama wouldn't allow him to come up to my bedroom.'

'No, Hetty. Surely you guessed it was me? I so much wanted to see you and I spoke to Ned and he arranged for Mary Fletcher to bring me.' The scarf was pulled down a little way.

Hetty exclaimed in delight, 'Sophia!'

'I have never before been away from the farm in my life,' Sophia whispered. 'The sights I have seen through this scarf today have been amazing. The world is more beautiful than I imagined.'

'You were very brave to come all this way to see me,' Hetty said, touched.

'Not as brave as you have been. Ned told me what you did and after that I thought it would be as nothing for me to visit.'

Perhaps now, Sophia would have the courage to show her face to the world in future, Hetty thought. She hoped so, and resolved that as soon as she was able to go about again, she and Mary Fletcher would encourage her. That was, if Mama ever let her out of her sight again.

★　★　★

It was two weeks later, when Hetty was allowed to leave her bed and sit in the salon beside a comforting fire against the winter chills, that she had another visitor.

Will Foster came into the room rather formally, as if he were unexpectedly shy.

'Your mother has not allowed me to

visit before,' he said. 'Though I have come to the house regularly to hear bulletins about your progress.'

'I'm nearly completely recovered now,' Hetty told him. 'No more than a trifling stiffness in my arm and the doctor says that will pass in time. I think I owe you thanks for bringing me safely home that night. I remember nothing after Abel fired his pistol.'

'The man escaped, but without the chest of valuables. He took my horse, but that has been recovered and will be returned safely in due course, along with Abel himself, who will face the Assizes in Maidenhead, together with two accomplices,' Will told her. 'Ned and I carried you back here and a fine tale we had to tell, or not to tell, to explain your presence in such a state.

'I think it best if you let your memories of that night remain confused and hazy. Did you really come to find us because you thought I was about to rob the coach, and you wanted to warn me that the Watch had been alerted?'

Hetty blushed. 'I thought — everything seemed to point to it. That lovely horse, hidden in the woods, and your cloak and pistols under the straw. I'm sorry, Will. I should have known you could not do anything like that.'

'You know the penalty for those who aid and abet highway robbers. And yet you still came to try to help me. Hetty, what am I to do with you? Here is a young woman who has no fears at all, it seems.

'Not only does she defy the dangers of leaping from a tree on to a moving haycart, and braves the darkness to ride out alone at night, but she puts herself in mortal danger by challenging a dangerous criminal, and saves my life by taking the bullet that would undoubtedly have struck me.'

'I couldn't let him shoot you,' Hetty whispered.

'And no more could I let such a woman escape from me. Hetty, I have come to ask you, will you do me the very great honour of consenting to become my wife?'

'Your wife?' Hetty stared at him, hardly understanding his words.

'I love you, Hetty. How could anyone not love anyone as brave and true as you? Please say you agree. I am not as brave as you, I would not have the courage to face our Sophia and have to tell her that I had not managed to persuade you to marry me.'

'That doesn't take any bravery,' Hetty said pertly. 'You had but to ask, Will Foster. You should have known I could not possibly refuse you. But you will have to gain permission from my stepfather, Sir John, first.'

'I have already asked his permission to speak to you.' Will hesitated, then added, 'He said — that perhaps I could make a better job of turning you into a young lady than he or your mother could ever do.'

'He said that?' Hetty sat up quickly, her eyes flashing angrily. Her shoulder twinged with the sudden movement and she lay back more cautiously.

'He also said — that in truth he would be sorry if you ever lost that spirit of yours. I had to reassure him that I hoped not, too.'

Hetty lay back on her couch, a great wave of happiness sweeping over her. Meg the gypsy had been right, totally right. She would be happy and content, though great riches would never be hers.

In a sense, though, she already had greater riches than would pay a king's ransom; Will, a sister in Sophia, and a farm that was already more like a home than Birch Hall had ever felt. She was completely happy.

THE END